HAMBURGERS & HOMICIDE

HAMBURGERS & HOMICIDE

POPPY'S FOOD TRUCK MYSTERIES #1

MOIRA BATES

FAWKES PRESS

1

The crunch of a keg rolling across gravel had become a comforting sound. A year ago, I would have laughed if anyone suggested I'd drop out of college to run a food truck on the grounds of St. Andrew's Brewery, and I never would have guessed it would make me happier than I've ever been.

Aaron slipped the empty keg into place, turning to face me with a smile. "What are you up to today, Pops?"

I rolled my eyes at the nickname but didn't correct him. Childhood friendship has privileges. "Kim and I are cleaning the outside walk-in, but we can't get to the top shelf. The stepladder is MIA—"

"No idea where it's gone, but I can help you." I had no doubts that his six-two frame could clear the top shelf before we could locate the missing ladder.

We reached the open door of the outside walk-in just in time to hear Kim exclaim, "Got it!" In one wild and glorious motion, she turned to display a crate triumphantly over her head before her makeshift method of elevation crumbled beneath her; boxes crushed, eggplant flew, potatoes rolled, and several quarts of heavy whipping cream swept off the shelf as Kim scrambled to find purchase. The entire mess landed on the wet floor with a sickening thud.

Aaron was already on the phone to 911 by the time I covered the short distance to Kim's side. Her body twisted at an unnatural angle, her eyes closed, and her jaw slack. "I..." the words came out in a hissed breath. "... found the... Japanese eggplant."

"I thought you were dead!" Laughter and tears fought for dominance, relieved my friend was alive and angry that she made me wonder.

Kim's eyes fluttered open, and she squinted against the light. "Not dead. Too much to do for Bluebonnet..."

"Don't think you're ridin' this year, Kim." Aaron pocketed his phone and knelt beside her.

"Not ridi—" we lost the rest to the wail of the siren as an ambulance bounced across the open lawn of the brewery to put all of Kim's pieces back together again.

"Gomez Family?" The doctor startled as a dozen people jumped from plastic chairs in the waiting room. "Are you *all* family?"

Andy, Kim's younger brother, stepped forward. He held his Stetson in his hands, his State Trooper uniform looking crisp despite the hours of hospital vigil. "No, ma'am, not technically. Kim is my sister, and most everyone else is related in the small-town sense. You'd just save me needing to repeat everything you say, if you'd say it to everyone."

"Well, I've got good news for you." We exhaled in unison and faces softened in relief. "But," The room quieted. "she's going to be here for a while, and off that leg for even longer." The doctor held up a tablet, flipping through x-ray images. "Concussion, but no skull fracture. A sprained shoulder, but again, no fractures. This," She stopped at an image that looked like a piece of splintered wood. "I don't even know how a person could do this from a fall—"

"It was a spectacular fall..." Aaron popped off, which earned a sharp look from me and a small moan from Kim's and Andy's elderly mother.

"I'm sure it must have been. The last time I repaired a leg like this, they had caught it between two cars." She turned off the tablet. "You should be thankful for that poor person, or I wouldn't have known what to do for your friend. As is, she's back together. She's not in any pain right now, but it will come later. She'll be here for at least a week, then we'll see how it's healing and release her home. It's a long road and she'll be taking it on crutches."

I STARED at the tasting flight Aaron slid across the bar. "I need to go back to the hospital."

"Andy told you to go home. He's the law, you have to do what he says."

I sniffed the first glass and pushed it away as the essence of sour laundry assaulted me. "Then why am I here?"

Aaron crossed his arms, leaning against the back counter. "Because Andy doesn't always know what he's talking about. Nobody but Kim's family needs to be up there right now. And you don't need to go home. One—you will get all mopey and blame yourself, and two—you will end up going back to the hospital."

"So, are you my babysitter?"

"More like babe-sitter, am I right?!" Aaron's 15-year-old brother crowed from across the room as he wiped down tables.

Aaron used an oft-practiced maneuver to hit the back of Cameron's head with a cardboard coaster. "Not cool, Cam, not cool."

"I'm sorry, Poppy, I didn't mean to show any disrespect."

I tried to look firm but knew he didn't mean any harm by it. Even after receiving a coaster to the noggin, he thought it was hilarious. Quite simply, fifteen is not an exceptional year for boys. Of course, based on my personal interactions with the male population, they seem to peak at about age eight, then become more unbearable with each passing year. "It's okay, Cam, now finish up those tables so you can help me clean up the scene of the crime."

"So..." Aaron pondered as he worked behind the bar. "How are you going to handle Bluebonnet Trails weekend without Kim?"

I crossed my arms and laid my head down on the bar. "I DON'T KNOW!" I screamed into the cocoon of flesh and polished wood. "Glebb... bill dumfum..."

"Pops? POPS?"

I lifted my face to see Aaron looking alarmed. "What?"

"Keep your head up. Literally, keep your head up. I can't understand anything you're saying."

I deflated. "I don't know what I'm going to do. It was going to be tough enough with just the two of us. There's nobody looking for work within a hundred miles. I can call my friend in Fort Worth, he might know—"

"He? Fort Worth? What?"

My gaze drifted to a couple standing outside the taproom windows, to Aaron, and back to the couple. They looked to be deep in discussion, but their body language made me uncomfortable. "Um, Roger. He runs a food truck park there. Anyway, maybe he would—are they okay?"

Aaron's head snapped to the window, and he bounded over the bar, charging out the door. "Hey, Sarah!" His tone was cheerful, but his voice strained. "You're late and we've got a lot of prep work tonight for the book club coming in!" He held the door open for her, then watched the man sulk away.

The young girl looked embarrassed, twisting her hands together as she stared at the floor. "I'm sorry, I thought I left—"

"Stop apologizing." Aaron resumed his place behind the bar. "Everything okay?"

She beamed as she glanced over her shoulder at her retreating partner. "Yes, it's good. I just forgot to tell Jake I was working tonight, and he made plans for us together... a misunderstanding. It's good now. Anyway, sorry to cause a fuss. I'll get to work."

She hustled off to the kitchen, Cam following, and the taproom fell silent.

"Hey, Pops...."

"Yes...." Aaron's seemingly innocent words sent alarm bells screaming in my head.

"I may have a solution to your problem."

"Okay..."

"Sarah—"

"Who is Sarah?"

He rolled his eyes and sighed. "*Sarah*. Sarah that was just standing here."

"Ah, okay. Sarah."

"We just hired her last week, and she mentioned the other day that she wants to go to culinary school. She wants to be a chef."

"Good luck, the competi—"

"Pops!" Aaron leaned across the bar. "You should talk to Sarah about filling in for Kim."

I opened the door to a timid knock. Sarah was ready for her first day of work; and the young man from outside the taproom was standing behind her.

"Jake's not staying," Sarah spilled out. "I just wanted to

introduce you guys. You didn't get the best impression of him the other day."

He had the good graces to dip his surfer blond head and blush. "I apologize, Ms. Price, it was important to me that Sarah hear what I was saying, and I let my emotions get the best of me." He lifted his face and offered a thousand-watt smile. "Sarah means the world to me." He squeezed her hand and shifted his gaze to her.

For a moment, I swore I was looking at the poster for a Nicholas Sparks movie. Two young lovers holding each other's gaze, bodies tilted together, the electricity of promised kisses in the air. Despite my dismal love life, I'm a sucker for romance. "You took the time to come out and set the record straight. That's the sign of a good man." I supposed so anyway... it seems like something my namesake, my great-grandfather Poppy, would have said. "Now, you're welcome back sometime, but right now, we have to get to work."

His smile flashed again, and I wondered how much his parents spent on orthodontics and teeth whitening. "You'll see me out front when you open. What's the special tonight?"

I laughed. "Nice try! You'll find out when the sign goes up. Now, leave my kitchen, please."

A wave and a kiss on Sarah's cheek and he left. Sarah gazed with hungry eyes around the workspace. For the first time since Kim's accident, I felt like things would be okay.

KEEPING MY EXPECTATIONS LOW, I chose Shrimp and Grits for the Friday night bar crowd. I watched as Sarah followed my recipe, tasting at each step and making tweaks to perfectly replicate the sample dish I had prepared earlier. "It should be," she explained, "the same batch to batch, but it's not. Sometimes the grits need just a smidge more cream, or a sprinkle of sugar to bring out the flavor."

Her dish was not as good as mine. Her dish was better. Placing my fork on the edge of the plate, I crossed my arms and faced her. "Please never leave me."

Sarah blushed at the roundabout praise. "I love working for you, but I know it is just until your regular assistant comes back."

"It doesn't have to be." Ideas rolled through my head. "Kim has never loved the weekend work. She'd rather handle the weekday morning crowd. You could take the weekend shift! And—" I bounced on my toes, excitement coursing. "We could even create to-go dinners for weekday evenings!"

Sarah's eyes lit up at the suggestion. "Ready-to-eat or heat-at-home?"

"What's got you ladies all hopped up?" Jake was at the door, ready to escort Sarah home.

"Poppy just offered to let me stay after her assistant comes back! We're going to do special dinners! It's goi—"

"Don't you think you are getting ahead of yourselves? It's only been one night." Jake squeezed Sarah's hand.

"Oh," she said, "maybe. I mean," She turned back to me. "We can talk more about it tomorrow." She brightened up. "Do you want me to grab some parsnips?"

"Yes," I said. "And come with ideas for Sunday. I'm thinking I might let you set the menu."

Jake hugged Sarah tightly. "Look at my girl! That's great."

Sarah beamed back at him. "It's all I've ever wanted."

Saturday's Bangers and Mash was a success, not in small part to Sarah's suggestion to grate parsnip into the potato mash and drizzle the roasted heirloom carrots with curry yogurt sauce. We sold out early in the night and had to switch to breakfast tacos to keep the food flowing until the taproom and local bars closed.

On Sunday, I did something I'd never done before. Something I had sworn never to do.

I turned the menu over to someone else.

A cooler full of duck and asparagus sat ready to be cooked to perfection, with a creamy citrus sauce to provide a light note and complement the richness of the duck. Instead, I handed it all to Sarah to show me what she could do.

Sarah twisted her hands and stared at the floor while I chewed. I followed the bite with a saltine cracker and a swallow of water. I closed my eyes, then took another bite. "Sarah?" I waited for her to lift her eyes, which were wet with unshed tears. "That is the best dish I've tasted in a long time. How did you decide on kebabs? And shaving the asparagus into wild rice is a genius move!"

"Yes," Sarah nodded. "I wanted to make the duck decadent and lighten it up with the salad."

"It is… amazing." I took another bite and moaned with pleasure. "You've got a bright future ahead of you."

The Sunday night crowds were heavier than the previous two nights, which had been insane. It took everything we had to keep up with orders—we even pulled Jake in the truck to help at the window. I'm not too proud to admit that I misjudged him that day at the taproom. Not only was he competent help in the kitchen, but his effusive charm was a big plus at the order window. He somehow made everyone feel like their order was the most special one of the night. I'm pretty sure I even heard him taking some orders in Spanish, which is impressive, since I often struggle with English—the only language I speak.

I stuffed the receipts from the weekend into my bag, too tired to worry about making a bank run. Exhausted, accomplished, and peaceful—everything was perfect.

～

C<small>ENTRAL</small> T<small>EXAS</small> only offers about a dozen days during the year when the morning and afternoon are equally pleasant to be outdoors. That meant twelve or so days I could walk the few blocks between the food truck and my home without risk of melting into a puddle. Ten minutes late for open, I increased my pace, torn between enjoying the morning and checking on Sarah as she opened the truck. I trusted Sarah to arrive on time, and if not, the regulars might have to wait a few minutes for coffee and breakfast tacos to flow out the window.

The scream of a siren interrupted my thoughts, taking me back to the day Kim had fallen. She was fine—well, as fine as you can be with a busted leg and a concussion—but I hoped never to see something like that again.

My hope wavered as I jogged across Fuller Street and saw an ambulance slide to a stop in front of the food truck. I picked up the pace, fearing that it might be one of my regulars. Mr. Flores had four stents put in last month—what if one failed? I scanned the crowd until I spied his face. I pushed my way through bodies and embraced him with fierce relief, as my mind had already gone to the worst-case scenario.

Or so I thought.

A tortured cry broke through the morning. "Sarah, no!"

I released my grip on Mr. Flores and pushed my way to the center of the crowd. Two men held a weeping and writhing Jake back as a paramedic covered Sarah where she lay still, gray, and with the handle of a 12-inch Wüsthof Classic chef's knife sticking out of her side.

I <small>SAT ON THE GROUND</small>, still damp with morning dew. The paramedics had transported Jake to the hospital for observation. Most of the crowd remained in a stunned silence. The Baseless PD, which consisted wholly of Chief Wilson and Officer

Cleary, interviewed those assembled. No one had seen it happen, but several had seen Sarah stumble out of the food truck before she collapsed on the ground. It had to have been a robbery, someone who thought the truck might hold the proceeds from the weekend. It didn't. We left $100 in the register to open. I shoved the rest of the cash from the weekend inside the extra slow cooker on the shelf in my garage since I'd been too tired to mess with a bank drop. A life was not worth $100. It wasn't worth any amount. Surely Sarah would have turned the money over without a fight?

"Do you understand?" Chief Wilson stared at me. "I need you to verbally acknowledge that you understand your rights."

"Excuse me?" I tried to focus on what he was saying. "I... could you repeat yourself?"

"Poppy Price, you are being arrested on suspicion of murder. You have the right to remain silent..." He lifted me from the ground and cuffed my wrists behind my back as he recited the Miranda Warning. "Do you understand?"

I looked around for help, or a sign that this was some kind of cruel prank. Many of my morning regulars watched in shock, and at least one person had their phone in the air, no doubt livestreaming the event. "No, I mean, yes. I understand my rights, but I don't understand why you are arresting me."

He shook his head and sighed. "I really don't have a choice when three different witnesses claim the victim only uttered one word—'Poppy.'"

2
———

Aaron chuckled under his breath.

"What?" I called from beneath the bar. "What are you laughing about?"

He stopped cleaning the mirror behind the bar, crossed his arms, and leaned against the wall. "We had to bail you out of jail."

I threw my sodden dishrag at him, but it landed at his feet with a squish. "You did not have to bail me out! There was no exchange of funds, no 'don't leave the country' talks, and they dropped the charges."

Aaron dropped the wet mess into the wash bucket and handed me a clean towel. "Because Andy convinced Wilson that you weren't a threat." His smile grew. "And to be fair, Wilson *did* tell you not to leave the area."

I gave up on cleaning and slumped against the bar. "I can't believe... I can't believe any of it. Why would I kill Sarah? Why would anyone kill Sarah? She was so sweet and talented. I wouldn't say this to just anyone, but she had a lot more natural talent as a chef than I do. She seemed to intrinsically understand what flavor profiles would pop, and how to coax an ingredient to the perfect texture. She could have been the next *Culinary Channel Star*."

"I don't know. It had to be a robbery—don't you think?"

"But nothing was taken." I glanced out the window where the food truck sat, yellow crime scene tape fluttering in the morning breeze.

"We think of Baseless as a small town, a safe place, but this close to the interstate," Aaron gestured east to I-35. "we're at the mercy of any freak who takes the exit. I hate to say it, but Sarah's killer is probably long gone."

"No," I sat up straighter, my mind clear for the first time since I saw Sarah's lifeless body. "That's not okay. I've worked hard on my business and I will not let it die along with Sarah. Rumors can kill my food truck and I will not let that happen."

Aaron narrowed his eyes. "There's nothing you can do. There's nothing any of us can do, except the police. Actually, there is something we can do—let's move on and have the biggest and best Bluebonnet Trails Bike Race weekend ever. We can honor Sarah's memory in that way."

I pointed to the food truck outside. "You might not have noticed the pretty yellow ribbon adorning the truck, but it says, 'CRIME SCENE—DO NOT CROSS'."

"Use our kitchen."

"Well, let's see…" I couldn't keep the sarcastic tone away. "My first assistant is laid up with a broken leg and concussion, and my second assistant is dead. I feel like I might have a hard time finding a third."

A noise at the door startled us. Wearing his uniform and Stetson hat, Trooper Andrew Gomez's silhouette made an imposing figure. Ever the gentleman, he removed his hat as he entered. "Hey, Poppy, I was hoping to find you here."

"Is it bad news? Just tell me. Get it over with."

"No," he shook his head. "I came to tell you that your truck will be released back to you this afternoon, so you'll be back in business soon." He frowned. "I want you to be ready for what you'll see—it's going to be a mess. CSU has covered virtually every surface in fingerprint powder, luminol, or both. I know how particular you are about keeping a neat kitchen, and it isn't going to be that way when you get it back. I'm sorry for that."

I stopped listening after he said I was getting my truck back. I was back in business.

~

KIM SOUNDED drowsy on the phone. "Why are you going there? Andy should do that."

"Sarah's roommate and Jake both said she didn't have any fam—"

"Who is Jake?"

"Sarah's boyfriend." I threaded between two 18-wheelers barreling down the interstate towards Austin. "Anyway, they both said she was a foster kid with no family. The police are trying to find her birth family, but that's complicated."

"Right," Kim yawned. "So, why are you going to some random address in Austin?"

"Because I think it might help find Sarah's family. She started writing it down on her W-9, like it was a habit, then marked through it. Call it a hunch, but it means something. If it's not her family, maybe it is someone who can help us find her family." The line was silent. "Kim? Don't you think? Kim?" The only response was the soft buzzing of a snore.

3

I drove slowly through the neighborhood. The narrow streets were lined with cars, and children played around them, oblivious to traffic. Muscle cars and luxury vehicles lined up nose to nose with rusted out hulls on blocks. My heart thudded, and I had a hard time imagining Sarah in this environment. Most of the houses were neatly kept, even though they'd seen better days. But the address Sarah had inadvertently given me? Well, I held my breath out of fear I might blow it down with a whisper.

A cracked sidewalk led from the street to the house with aluminum foil on the windows winking in the afternoon sun. With great care, I tapped lightly on the door. There was no response, so I tapped a bit louder. I could hear movement, a low murmur of voices. I turned away from the door, then stopped. I returned to the door and gave three loud knocks and called out, "Hello, I'm looking for a young lady you might know."

A moment later I could hear locks being turned and chains dropped, and the door opened to a thin woman I guessed to be in her mid-thirties. Her make-up was heavy and smudged, the marks where she had picked at her face still visible. I peered beyond her to see mattresses on the floor, bodies in various states of dress draped across them. Empty takeout boxes, bottles, and lighters littered the place. She spoke and her teeth confirmed my fears.

"Can't help you without a name."

"Sarah," I gathered my wits and tried to push away the idea that Sarah could have been a drug user. "I'm looking for someone who knows Sarah."

"Sorry, honey," she started to close the door. "I don't know any Sarah, so we have no business together."

"Wait!" I pulled my phone from my pocket and frantically scrolled for a picture of Sarah proudly holding up her plated duck kebabs. "Her! Do you know her?"

"Hey!" The woman pushed the door open wider and shouted past me to the kids in the street. "You know the deal —stay away from the cars that have business here." The kids mumbled and skulked away from my car. Her glassy eyes tried to focus on the picture. "Oh, hey, Cookie! How's she doing?"

"Did Sarah—umm, *Cookie*—live here? Is she family?"

"She was here for a few months." The woman fumbled a cigarette into her mouth. "Name wasn't Sarah though… Molly, I think, was what she called herself. We called her Cookie because she spent more time in the kitchen than anywhere else."

"Do you know where I could find her family?"

The woman blew a ring of smoke and laughed. "You're looking at 'em. Foster kid who ran as soon as she turned eighteen. She was staying here because she didn't have family, didn't want family. She's not in any kind of trouble, is she? She's a sweet kid—"

I took a deep breath and dropped my voice. "She's dead."

∾

I WANDERED AIMLESSLY through the restaurant supply, ostensibly there to pick up supplies for the weekend. I was really using the familiar setting as a place to clear my mind and think about Sarah.

The home I visited was obviously a trap house, by the looks of the occupants, probably dealing in methamphetamines. Sarah had shown no signs of drug use, past or present, and the hallmarks of meth use—the pox from picking at skin and teeth rotting from the bottom—don't exactly disappear as soon as you stop using. She could have been a dealer, but that seems so out of character for her. And if she was selling, but not using, why leave? There is no doubt drugs are a profitable business.

Beyond that, who was she? She presented a valid ID with the name Sarah Brown when I hired her. At least, it appeared to be valid, with all the anti-counterfeiting measures in place. The address was an apartment in Baseless, so according to the timeline from the woman at the house, Abigail, it had to have been issued in the last six months. How does one gain a new identity virtually overnight?

So far, the only things consistent were Sarah's desire to attend culinary school and her time in the foster system. Her name, her family, her past—all a mystery.

"Hey, Poppy!" the manager, Alex, called across the store. "Finding everything you need for the Bluebonnet crowds?"

I nodded and started to extract myself from the conversation when the pieces snapped together. "Yep, I need to hire more help." I pulled up the photo of Sarah I had shown Abigail. "She used to live around here."

He looked at my phone. "Oh, sure!" He thought for a moment. "Molly! It's been ages since she's been in. Such a sweet kid, but she didn't have a restaurant affiliation. I shouldn't have given her a membership card, but she was so eager... she loved to talk about food. Good to see she's finally getting her break—she'll make a great addition to your truck."

~

"CAN YOU DO THAT?"

Kim sighed. "I don't know. I can try, but finding information is a lot more difficult when you're bed bound and on drugs."

It took all I had not to scream. "It was an accident!"

"I know! It wasn't even your fault. If I hadn't been so impatient and just waited for the Jolly Red Giant to come help us—"

"He hates it when you call him that."

"I know, but I get a pass on things like that right now. There aren't many perks to my situation but speaking freely is one of them."

"So how will you find the info?"

I heard the rapid click of Kim hitting the button on the drug delivery system for her pain medication. "Oh, I don't know. I guess I'll start the old-fashioned way with Google. Maybe a reverse image search? In the end, I'll ask Andy and he'll tell me to stay out of it. I'll remind him that he never would have conquered 4th grade without me, and he'll throw me a bone." Her words slurred, the medication taking effect. "It would help if you had any real info—"

"This is Trooper Andrew Gomez, to whom am I speaking?" The sudden boom of Andy's voice cut through my car.

"Andy," I did my best to sound cheerful and concerned. "I was just checking in on Kim. How's she doing?"

"She's asleep." His tone brooked no nonsense. "What are the two of you up to?"

"Nothing. Just checking in. That's it."

"She was talking about 4th grade. She only talks about 4th grade when she's going to ask me for a favor—usually one I can't grant. And often when the two of you are up to something."

"Andy, I assure you no one is up to anything."

The line was silent for a moment. "We will find out who killed Sarah. I'd consider it a personal favor if you'd stay out of trouble so that we only have the one crime to focus on."

I vacillated between anger and thankfulness. I knew he was sincere and concerned, but he couldn't help but come off a little smug. "Thanks, Andy. You do your job and I'll do mine."

I ended the call as I pulled up to the food truck, crime scene tape gone, doors open, and people everywhere.

Heart pounding, I threw the car in park and jumped out. "What's going on?" I struggled to maintain even breathing.

"Oh, hey, Poppy!" Mrs. Melvin came out of the truck carrying a bus tub full of supplies. "We were hoping to get this finished before you got back."

I stared at her, trying to fathom why my childhood friend's mother would be in my recently-a-crime-scene food truck. "Why... what..." I noticed they had covered the ground with tarps and the contents of my truck. "I do—"

"Pops!" Aaron crunched across the gravel, holding one end of a cooler laden with drinks. Our friend Ben held the other end up.

They dropped the cooler and Ben engulfed me in a massive hug. I squeezed him back, along with the tears that threatened at his appearance. "What are you doing here?" I choked out.

"Wow," He stepped back in mock surprise. "No 'So good to see you, Ben!'? Rude."

Mrs. Melvin scowled. "Ben! She's been through a lot—behave yourself!"

"Mom!" I had witnessed a variation of this scene dozens of times growing up. "It's Poppy—she knows. It's okay." He smiled at me. "I'm always going to be here when she needs a friend, and I'm always going to give her a hard time about it."

I motioned to my life's work spread about on the ground. "Why are you ransacking my truck?

Mrs. Melvin laughed. "We're not ransacking your truck, we're cleaning! Aaron told Ben what was going on, and Ben told me, and—" she gestured widely. "word got around. Everyone wanted to help get it clean and back in order for you. You've been through enough."

"Oh." The tears threatened again.

"It's okay," she reached out to touch my arm. "Why don't you go have a break in the taproom while we finish up? We'd hoped you would spend a little longer in Austin."

I nodded, following Aaron and Ben back to the taproom. I was immensely grateful for the group of volunteers, most of whom I didn't even know, who spent their afternoon removing all evidence that anything was ever amiss. I was also unfathomably sad that Sarah's impact was so fleeting that they could wipe it away with a damp sponge and some elbow grease.

4

"Only in Baseless would being a crime scene double your business." I flopped on the floor of the food truck, the remains of the morning's rush all around me.

Aaron grabbed two drinks and sank to the floor beside me. "I dunno. Seems like it is human nature for people to be fascinated by crime. How else do you explain all the death row inmates with people lining up to marry them?"

"I guess I can understand people being curious, but I haven't been this busy in weeks."

"Or," Aaron postulated. "maybe the short time without access to your food reminded people how much they love it. Absence makes the heart grow fonder and all that."

I pulled myself up and started to clean the counter. "Yep, there's no other place in central Texas you can buy a breakfast taco."

Aaron laughed and joined me in cleaning. "Speaking of… I don't ask for much, but since I'm not getting paid…"

"Coming up." I turned the grill back on and grabbed some tortillas. "I really appreciate you helping this morning. There's no way I could have made it through this morning without help, and I'm sure lunch will be about the same."

"What are you going to do tomorrow?"

I flipped the sizzling bacon. "I don't know. I'm back in the same situation—everyone is already gearing up for Blue-bonnet weekend. I guess I'm back to calling Roger."

Aaron snorted. "I'm sure there is someone who isn't spoken for. Ask Ben's mom for help."

"It's a big weekend for her cat rescue group. She and all her friends are booked." I added a squirt of homemade salsa to Aaron's breakfast taco and handed it to him. "Besides, as great as she is, I'm not sure she understands 'working with'—she's a bit of a force. Right now, I really just need someone who can follow directions."

Aaron swallowed a bite of his taco and smiled. "I'm sure you'll figure it out, and the bright side is that you will be too busy to dwell on Sarah and her past. It sounds like she's not who we thought she was, and I don't want you getting involved in that mess."

I took a large bite of my own breakfast to avoid answering.

Locking the food truck on my way out, I hesitated and popped back in to grab the plastic wedge doorstop and an extra-long wooden chopstick. I knew that priority number one needed to be finding someone to help in the truck, but I couldn't get the house in Austin out of my mind.

Sarah had lived in an apartment on the edge of town. The complex was popular with students at a local college, so a weekday afternoon found it virtually empty. I wasn't sure what my plan was. Actually, I didn't have a plan, just a yearning to find something, anything, that would answer my questions about Sarah.

I spotted what I thought was her car, an older model sedan in a sickly green color. I'd only seen her in it once, so I wasn't one hundred percent sure it was even hers. But, if she'd been in it, it might hold a clue. I pulled into a visitor spot across the lot and threw my bag over my shoulder, trying to look like I was just another student on my way to visit a friend.

I pulled out my phone as I stood by the car, hoping anyone who saw me would think I had just stopped to answer a text. I glanced through the passenger window at the contents of the car. Despite the rough exterior, the inside was clean, with few personal items. After determining I was as hidden as I could possibly be in a wide-open parking lot bathed in April sunshine, I thanked heaven for the propensity of weekend partiers to locking keys in their cars. I had never expected to need to know how to break into a car, but I was certainly glad for the skill. I quickly inserted the edge of the doorstop in between the door and the car's frame and gave it two hard taps with my fist. A small gap opened, and I slipped the chopstick in, clicking the lock open before depositing the chopstick and doorstop back in my bag. Baseless should be glad that I use my powers for good. Or, at least, not for evil. This particular use might fall into a gray area, but definitely not evil.

I pulled on a pair of kitchen gloves and opened the door. A faint smell of stale cigarette smoke wafted out. The sickly sweet floral scent of an air freshener popped in the vent followed it. I'm not sure which was worse, but both added to the reasons I didn't want to spend more than the absolute minimum of time necessary in the car. I opened the glove box knowing that a person who got into mine could probably rebuild my life with the ephemera inside. Instead, I found the required insurance liability card from a fly-by-night company. It had her name—or one of them—and the address of this apartment. There was no car registration, or random receipts, or extra fast-food straws. Sticking my hand deep into the crevices, I pulled out a crushed pack of gum and a piece of paper with "76432" written on it. I snapped a picture and placed everything back in the glove box.

The parking lot remained quiet, so I reached below the seats, hoping for a score. Under the passenger seat I found two empty energy drink cans. The space beneath the driver's seat was empty, but the black hole of every car—the slight space between the driver's seat and the center console—promised a slip of paper. I tried to slip my hand in to retrieve it, but only managed to push it farther into the abyss. Of course, it wasn't quite far enough to reach it from the bottom. I pulled the chopstick from my bag and angled it to press the paper against the hard plastic of the center console. I inched it up slowly, freeing it. It was half an envelope. There was no letter inside, but the envelope bore the embossed return address of the First Family Free Fellowship in Waco. From what remained, it looked like they had addressed it to someone named Case, probably in this apartment complex.

Defeated, I snapped a picture and dropped the paper back in place. I'd risked getting caught to find absolutely nothing. I shoved the used gloves into my bag and carefully backed out of the car and into Jake.

I yelped in surprise, both from Jake and the almost simultaneous appearance of a Baseless PD cruiser. Well, *the* Baseless PD cruiser.

Officer Cleary rolled his window down and peered out at me. "Poppy? What are you doing over here? This car is evidence. That don't look so good with the victim's last word being your name."

Jake stepped forward. "I asked her to come over. It helps to talk about Sarah with friends and this, well, I know this is just part of the investigation, but it's hard." His voice quavered with emotion.

Cleary stepped out of his car, waving at the tow truck that had entered the parking lot. He made a noise that might have been acceptance. "Whatcha' doin' with the door open?"

Jake jiggled a set of keys. "Just getting it ready for the truck. It's a lot easier if you can drop it into neutral."

"Be that as it may, the two of you are still getting all over our evidence."

I inched away from the car my it's-only-a-felony-if-you-get-caught kit tucked close to my body. "I thought the DPS was running the investigation."

The officer stood taller and scowled. "We're cooperatin' in a joint investigation. Just because they have all the crime labs and stuff don't mean they get to run the show. It's our juris-diction. Chief Wilson says he'll be damned if they are going to stick their noses in on this one."

"Oh, well that makes sense," I kept my voice light. "I'm sure you guys will do a great job. I'm a big supporter of Base-less PD." I took a step toward my car, calling me like a flashing beacon on a dark night. "I'll get out of your way, so you can get to work."

"Hang on, Poppy," Jake had handed the keys off to the tow truck driver and re-appeared by my side. "Let's finish our talk. We can sit by the grill pits over there just in case these guys need anything else from us."

My heart raced, and I hoped that my guilty flush was not spreading up my neck and face. Trapped, I had no choice. "Sure, let's have a seat while they finish."

The table at the grill pit sat no more than 30 feet from Sarah's car, but it felt like the March of Bataan. My legs became more leaden with every step as I alternated thanking higher powers that the police hadn't caught me and wondering how in the world I could explain myself to Jake. We settled at the table and sat in silence for a full two minutes. Or seven days, I could no longer tell.

Finally, Jake broke the silence. "Well?"

"I'm really sorry that you are going through this. Sarah was special."

He stared at me as if I'd sprouted an arm from my forehead. "Thank you, but that's not what this is about. What were you doing in Sarah's car and why shouldn't I turn you in to Barney Fife over there?"

"I—" My brain suddenly powered back on. "Why *didn't* you turn me in? You definitely caught me in her car, and my name was the last thing she said."

His laugh caught me off guard. "Wow, it's a good thing you are a chef and not a defense attorney!" He glanced over his shoulder at the men fiddling with the settings on the tow truck. "Because I know, well, I *think*, that you didn't kill her. You were the first person to really see her talent and offer her a chance."

"Which is exactly why some people suspect me—they think I was jealous."

He leaned across the table, his expensive teeth flashing in the late afternoon sun. "If you get arrested, please don't say anything. You are *really* bad at this." He sighed and leaned back. "Did you kill her?"

"No."

"I believe you. Now, why were you in her car, and how did you get in?"

Unable to come up with a somewhat believable lie, I took a path that had become foreign of late. "I'm trying to find out more about who Sarah was. I think it might lead us to who killed her."

Jake's brow wrinkled in concern. "What do you mean 'who Sarah was'? Did you find something?"

I shook my head in defeat. "No, but I know her name wasn't Sarah."

The words were whispered. "How did you find out?"

"I found Abigail in Austin. She told me that Sarah's name was really Molly." I pressed on the pain in my temples. "Why do you think she changed it? Was she in trouble? In drug trouble?"

"Oh, not Sarah," Jake's laugh was mirthless. "No, she just

needed a place to stay. She bounced out of foster care with no money, no family, and was living on the streets. I'm not sure how she ended up at that trap house, but she said she got out as soon as she could. She met Larissa in Austin and had an opportunity to move up here when Ris came to school."

"Did you know Sarah then?"

"No," he paused, as if watching a film in his head. "we didn't get together until after we'd both moved here." He let out a breath and the next words rushed from his mouth. "I had some trouble, a little too much fun partying in Lubbock. My Christmas present from my parents was 45-days in rehab. After that, they thought I needed a fresh start, so here I am." He lifted his arms from his sides. "I met Sarah and thought it had all been worth it to wind up in the same place she had. She hated living in the trap house—she saw a lot of bad stuff go down. She was happy to be with someone working the program to stay clean. Sarah was amazing, and I knew she'd never let me go down that path again. It was good."

I watched the taillights of the squad car as it followed the tow truck out of the parking lot. "I'm sorry. Sounds like life dealt her a bad hand and she was just trying to improve it." I sighed and stood from the table. "Thanks for not turning me in, but I've got to go. I've got about... oh... twelve hours to hire a new assistant."

"I'm sure you've got a lot of people who'd love to work for you."

"You'd think so, right?" The injustice and humor collided. "I mean, one assistant broke her leg on my watch, and the other got murdered, it's not like things are going to get worse. What does a person have to lose?" I sighed. "In all honesty, the Bluebonnet Trails Bike Race is the biggest event in the I-35 corridor. Everyone who can work is already spoken for, not just in Baseless, but for 100 miles in either direction."

"Not everyone."

"That's what I'm hoping...."

"Poppy." Jake raised one eyebrow. "Right here. I'm not in school this semester. I'm 're-acclimating' and attending NA meetings. I've been Sarah's *sous* a lot—I know all the grunt work, from dicing onions to washing dishes."

I looked at him for a solid minute before speaking. Could the answer be that easy? "The hours are horrible, and the pay isn't much better."

"Right, and I really should suspect you of Sarah's murder. Got it."

Relief washed across me. "Really, would you help me get through the rest of this month?"

He extended his hand for me to shake. "I'm available as long as you need me. Well, until the next semester starts. No offense, but my parents would have a meltdown if I decided to quit school and work in a food truck."

I laughed as I shook his hand. "Believe me, I know!"

"And Poppy?" He hadn't let go of my hand. "I also want to know what happened to Sarah. Partners?"

I gave his hand another squeeze. "Partners."

5

It was official, spring was morphing into summer at a rapid pace. Sweat dripped off the end of my nose as I stood in front of the fan. Jake stood with his face in the cooler. "Is it always this hot?"

"Yes," I replied, "but not always so miserable. I have a/c, but I don't usually turn it on until I can no longer stand the heat in the kitchen—literally. If I turn it on in April, it feels like nothing in August—"

A voice came from the service window. "And the humidity doesn't help."

"That's the truth!" Andy stood before me in shorts and a t-shirt, a stark departure from the highly starched khaki uniform he usually wore. "What are you up to today, Andy?"

"Kim was released, so I'm staying at the house with her, and of course, Mom and Dad. I made breakfast, and they all asked that I please come to you to pick up some lunch. They're a picky bunch."

"Any special requests?" I knew the answer and started assembling ingredients before he could reply.

"Nope, Kim said, 'Poppy will know.'" He tilted his head to see into the truck. "Hi, Mr. Bailey, are you Poppy's shadow now? Officer Cleary told me you were together when he went to pick up Sarah's car."

Jake shook his head with a small laugh. "I guess you could say that. Poppy needed an assistant, and I needed something to take my mind off what happened to Sarah, so here I am." He paused for a moment. "And, please, call me Jake."

Andy nodded. "Of course, when I'm off duty." I noticed he didn't offer reciprocal familiarity.

I kept my voice light and betrayed the curiosity I felt. "Did they find anything helpful in the car? I'll feel so much better when they catch whoever did it."

Andy smiled and leaned against the counter. "You know I can't talk about an ongoing investigation."

I stopped my work and gave him a knowing stare. "But you are off duty and can gossip all you want."

Jake removed himself from the conversation and continued to work around me.

Andy sighed. "Completely off-the-record and unofficially, no, there was nothing useful in the car. We still haven't been able to find her family, or any record of her in the foster care system. More than a murder, we've got a Jane Doe."

Jake re-entered the conversation. "What do you mean by that? We know she is... who she was."

Andy glanced around to make sure we were alone. "No, we don't. She's got documents in her name, but it turns out that none of them are legal. They are all fantastic fakes. Her roommate says that when she first met her, she was going by the name Molly."

Jake and I both gasped and pasted shocked looks on our faces.

"That's not possible!" Jake spit out. "I mean, she told me she used to go by Molly, but Sarah—that was her real name, her real identity."

"Why would she do something like that?" I asked. "I mean, create a fake identity—"

"I don't know, but it sure is making things complicated. Robbery-gone-wrong by someone who came off the interstate is still the most likely scenario, but we can't be sure until we find out who she really was." Andy reached for his wallet. "What's the damage?"

I pushed the large bag to him. "Nothing today. Give my love to all, especially Mami and Papi."

"Thanks, Poppy, I will. Stop by soon. They miss you and Kim needs someone else to drive crazy for a while."

As we watched Andy carefully belt the food into the front seat, Jake asked, "Are you related to him?"

"Who? Andy? No. Why would you think that?"

"You just seem very familiar—you called his parents *Mami y Papi*." With his practiced intonation the names sound like a native Mexican speaker, unlike my Texas drawl, which added extra syllables.

"We grew up just down the street from each other, so I've known his family forever. At some point they stopped being Mr. and Mrs. Gomez and became Papi and Mami. Our special salsa? They helped me create the recipe. They've always been supportive of my dream to be a chef."

What I didn't tell him was that, for a time, they were the only ones supportive of my dream. Most of my family didn't see it as a serious career—or they didn't think I had the talent to make it a serious career. I would still be stuck in school trying to earn a degree in something that didn't interest me if it hadn't been for my namesake, my Poppy. He'd always believed in me and encouraged my passion for cooking, even driving me to the State Fair in Dallas as a kid to compete against other aspiring young chefs. Win or lose, he would tell me, "It's all part of your ten-thousand hours, kid."

The Big-C took my great-grandfather away. In those last few months, I spent as much time with him as I could. He couldn't eat more than a few bites at a time, and often it had to be pureed, but he still wanted me to cook for him. He said it fed his soul, and it certainly fed mine. We talked for hours in those final days about what I wanted out of life, how I could see my way to my dream. That's when the idea of a food truck first materialized. I don't know who mentioned it first, but it came from the magic of the two of us together. His mind, still sharp, was designed for business. He led me through creating a business plan, estimating costs, and all the non-cooking aspects of the dream. I had hoped that once I finished college, I could get a job that would allow me to put away enough money to reach that dream.

But my Poppy had other ideas. To each of his six great-grandchildren, he left a sum of money to be spent on their dream. From debt-free college to spending the summer on an archaeological dig to my food truck, the bequests were specific to our personal goals. There were also bequests to the rest of the family, to be issued in one year, provided there had been no interference with how the great-grandchildren spent their money. To say that my parents had a meltdown was on the scale of saying Texans like chips and queso, when in truth, it is one of the four main food groups. (The other three being barbecue brisket, Dr. Pepper, and tacos.)

But, in the end, my Poppy had spoken. Six (very) young adults scattered to the winds to live our dreams, undeterred, for one full year. Except for me. I stayed right where I was, because I wanted my dream to be on full display for all of my family, all of Baseless, to see. The year was almost up, and things were booming. Well, except for the small issue of keeping assistants. But every morning and lunch time found a line of eager customers for my standard fare. It paid the bills and then some. But weekends—that was the magic. I could have catered to the bar crowd with nachos and hot wings, but instead, I created dishes only found on my menu, and only for one night. *Texas Monthly* had called me out in an article entitled "Hidden Texas Gems," and then things really went crazy. I had calls for catering gigs as far away as Dallas, but I tended to only take them from people in Baseless, being a huge believer in "dance with who brung ya."

That's why, with all that was happening, I couldn't just walk away. I couldn't close the truck. I couldn't miss the Blue-bonnet Trails weekend. I couldn't let my truck become known as the place where Jane Doe was murdered. I had to make it work for my Poppy. He believed in me.

I PEEKED out the window to make sure no customers were headed across the lot before flipping the sign to "closed."

Jake had his face in the cooler again. I tossed him a dish-cloth that I had dunked in ice water. "You might want to wear short sleeves tomorrow. It's going to be even hotter."

His face flushed even more red, and he dipped his eyes to the floor. "I'd rather not." He took a deep breath and met my curious gaze. "You know I told you about my... problems? I have some scars and marks that are still visible. That's not who I am anymore, and I don't want people to get the wrong impression."

I felt like a fool, even though I'd have had no way to know the situation. "Of course, I understand! You don't have to be ashamed of who you were—you're past that—but if the thought of explaining it to people makes you uncomfortable, then you do you. I will support your decision, either way."

"Thanks, Poppy." He smiled and I once again wondered about his perfect teeth, especially if he'd had a drug problem. I'm pretty sure being the daughter of a dentist was supposed to afford me some privilege, but it seems like my biggest take-away was an unnatural obsession with teeth. If I were ever attacked, I probably couldn't tell you male or female, race, size, or anything relevant—but I'm sure I could tell you about the condition of their teeth.

"No worries, now let's get out of this oven."

Jake seemed to hesitate. "Do you… do you think that trooper was honest about what they found in the car?"

"Yes," I nodded emphatically, "there wasn't anything useful in the car."

He arched an eyebrow. "Oh, really?"

It was my turn to blush. "This," I pulled out my phone to show the two pictures I had taken. "is all I found, and neither one of them tells me anything. What about you?"

He flipped by the picture of the torn envelope. "Churches are always sending stuff to students in those apartments. I think they buy a mailing list from the management or something. Anyway, it was probably just trash from someone else's mail." He stopped at the picture of the five digits and studied in intently. "This—is this a zip code?

"Yes!" I grabbed my phone out of his hands and stopped myself before I hugged him. "It's got to be a zip code. I wonder if it can help us find Sarah's family?"

"Maybe," he said, "You should probably tell that trooper."

"Well…." I weighed the idea of telling Andy I had been poking around in Sarah's car. "I left the paper right where I found it. So, technically, they already have it. If it leads to anything, then I'll tell Andy. He's much more likely to forgive me if I have a real lead."

Blanket, Texas.

It wasn't that far away, and I'm pretty sure I must have driven through it at some point, but I couldn't remember it. Nestled just off 377, it was a blip on the map with a few thousand people. I pulled up the website for the local paper, but it was primarily garage sale ads and school sports stats. *Schools!* I found the site for the local high school and started trawling through the pages. School lunch menus, more sports stats, reminders to buy prom tickets.... I tried entering "Molly" into the search bar. I found one science teacher, the president of the drama club, and an ad for a real estate agent. Sarah landed more results, but even less useful information, if possible. An English teacher, the attendance registrar, 2 girls in FCA, and one Sarah each in a half-dozen other clubs. Not exactly the hot lead I was looking for.

~

I FOUND myself knocking on the door of Sarah's apartment, her last paycheck in my hand.

The door cracked open, and Sarah's roommate peeked out. "Yes?"

"Hi, Larissa—it is Larissa, right?" I was already sounding like somebody there to sell religion or cosmetics or both. "I think we met at the truck once. I'm Poppy—Sarah was working for me—"

"Yes?" She could not have displayed her irritation more if she'd been holding a sign that said 'go away.'

"So, I have her last paycheck, but I don't know where to send it. I thought you might know—"

"I don't."

"But you knew her when she was Mol—"

The crack in the door widened and Larissa stepped into the hallway, clicking the door behind her. Her voice dropped to a whisper. "Look, I don't know what you think you know, but you do not want to get involved with this. She was living in a trap house with a bunch of meth heads. 'Molly' said she wanted to come here with me to break away, but I'm not sure she did. Changing her name didn't make her a different person."

"Do you... do you think she was involved in drugs?"

"I think she was dealing with some bad people and that is how she ended up dead."

"Do the police know—"

"Look, I've told them everything I know." She turned her back to me, quickly entering a code to open the door, and stepped back into the apartment. "I'm sorry she's dead, but she made her decisions and got what was coming to her."

The door clicked shut, and she left me standing in the hallway wondering what had just happened.

THE TAPROOM BUZZED with conversation when I arrived. I wanted to talk to Aaron about the possibility of drugs in Baseless. Weed was pretty widely available, even if it wasn't legal, and you'd get the occasional person addicted to prescription drugs after an accident or surgery. But anything else? Not in Baseless. It wasn't Mayberry RFD, but it was pretty dang close. People joked that there was no sin in Baseless, but everyone knew how to get there and back before dark. It wasn't far from the truth.

As soon as it was determined I wasn't anyone important, the hushed whispering resumed. I made my way through the tables and found Aaron at the end of the bar. He motioned me through the swinging doors to the kitchen. "I don't think I can stand this, but I can't kick them out!"

"Why are they so glum? It feels like someone died."

Aaron stared at me. "You haven't heard." It wasn't a question, but a statement. "Rhys Gilley, up at the high school. They think it was an overdose."

My heart leapt into my throat. "What? That's not possible. That doesn't happen—"

"Just like murder doesn't happen in Baseless?" Aaron peeked out at the hushed crowd. "Face it, Pops, the world is changing, and not for the better."

"How did it happen?"

"He didn't show up for the team bus to the baseball game. Coach sent somebody over to his house and they found him. Sixteen-years-old, strong, smart—and dead because of drugs." He slammed his fist on the wall.

I touched his shoulder. "How is Cam taking it?" Although a certified pain-in-the-patootie, Aaron's little brother meant the world to him.

"Not well," He sighed and pulled his hands through his coppery hair. "He knew him, but they didn't run in the same circles. Rhys was older, but all the JV kids look up to the ones on Varsity. They're…. I don't know, *aspirational*. You remember that age—invincibility is the name of the game. You think nothing can hurt you, and you sure don't think anything can hurt the ones you look up to." He pushed through the kitchen doors to take his place behind the bar. "But I can tell you one thing—whoever brought that poison into Baseless better get out before everyone figures out who did it. And we *will* figure it out."

6

"I may have something." Kim was more like her old self again. The only difference was that instead of buzzing around like a highly caffeinated insect, I settled her into a large chair with her leg propped up in front of her. Her petite, 5'2" frame looked even smaller in the massive cushions that surrounded her. She spun her laptop screen to face me. "Here. The church."

I gazed at a picture of the brick structure, the site peppered with links to nourish your spiritual being and fill their coffers. "Yep, that's the same logo that was on the envelope."

She clicked on "about us" tab and pulled up a picture of the "First Family Free Fellowship." *Hmmph*. That's what my solidly Methodist mother would refer to as *suspiciously New Age*. "This," Kim poked her finger at the screen, "is Pastor Harold Jones, Mother Arianna Jones, and their two children." I looked at the photo. The entire family was dressed in white, stiffly posed and surrounded by vases of red flowers. The effect was something along the lines of Olan Mills meets Stephen King. "Who is missing," Kim scrolled down the page, "is their 'eldest, Casey, who is away at college.'"

"So?" I wondered if the pain pills had muddled her mind, even though her speech was clear.

Kim flopped her head against the cushions and slapped the arm of the chair. "Because. Casey. Jones. Knows. Larissa. Fielding."

My mind roiled. "How? How do you know? Where is Casey now?"

I heard Kim's printer whirring as it kicked out a small stack of documents. Fueled by muscle memory, she started to rise to retrieve them, then settled back with a heavy sigh. She waved in the general direction of her desk. "Please?"

I retrieved the stack of papers and waited, impatiently, as Kim shuffled through them. She extracted one and handed it to me, a satisfied smile on her face. It was an article from a Lubbock-area newspaper, and it included a picture of two mangled vehicles, pieces scattered across the roadway.

A young father is in critical condition following a two-vehicle crash in rural Hockley County. Official reports conclude that Dustin Bennett, 27, was changing his tire on the side of the road when his vehicle was struck by a late model Dodge Challenger driven by an unnamed 16-year-old. The force of the impact tossed him into the roadway, and he sustained multiple broken bones and internal bleeding.

The 16-year-old driver and a 15-year-old passenger were both transported to the hospital with minor injuries. Both have been charged with a curfew violation, and the driver is being investigated for driving under the influence.

As I finished reading, she slipped another article into my hands.

Dustin Bennett remains in critical condition following the two-vehicle crash last week on Carpenter Road in Hockley County. Doctors expect him to survive but are unsure if he will regain use of his legs. A fundraiser has been set up to assist with expenses for his family, which includes a 3-year-old daughter, and a wife who is preparing to deliver their second child any day.

It is the practice of this paper not to share identifying information regarding juveniles unless officials charge them with a felony. Felony charges are not sealed in juvenile court, but are part of the open records in criminal court. Both state and federal courts recognize as wholly legal release of such information.

Larissa Fielding,16, has been charged with Intoxication Assault and Driving Under the Influence, as well as a curfew violation. The Dodge Challenger was a gift to celebrate her birthday earlier in the week. After a night of drinking in her home, she and her 15-year-old friend took it out to "test it on the back roads." At this time, the 15-year-old has not been charged with anything other than a curfew violation, so will remain unnamed.

Calls to Fielding's attorneys had not been returned by press time.

I snatched the third page from Kim's hand. It was a montage of social media posts from the day of the accident. Messages posted to Larissa's social media. "Praying for you, gurl!" "Love you Ris and Casey" "Just heard the news—so sorry about your car!"

Over and over, it referenced Casey as the second person in Larissa's car during the accident.

"I don't get it," I handed the paper back to Kim. "Who is Casey and how is she… he? How are they connected to Sarah?"

Kim furrowed her brow. "I'm not sure. It might not mean anything. But, if Sarah's roommate knew this Casey before she came to Baseless, and she knew Sarah when she was Molly, maybe this Casey person did, too. They might know who Sarah really was."

Kim's daughters interrupted our investigative efforts coming in the front door. The youngest, 10-year-old Lexi, immediately ran to show me the library book she had checked out. We discussed the premise of the book, focusing on whether a mermaid dragon was one step too far to suspend belief when reading. "How can they breathe fire underwater?" Lexi questioned, and honestly, I wanted to know myself.

Her oldest daughter, Gabi, was 14 and a freshman at Baseless High School. She offered a weak smile and headed straight to her room. "Gabrielle," Kim called after her, "how are things at school?"

She slunk back around the corner and dropped her bag. "Bad. They had counsellors today. But it's weird. A lot of us didn't know him, so it feels wrong to go to the counsellor, but it still... I don't know. It's not good."

"Aww, *bébé*," Kim waved her daughter over to her and stroked her hair. "It's okay. The counsellors are there for everyone. Your school has been turned upside down with this, it is normal to feel all out of sorts."

"I know," Gabi laid her head against Kim's shoulder. "And Tio is there—usually that embarrasses me, but today it made me feel good. I know he won't let me be somewhere that isn't safe."

Kim deposited a kiss on the top of her head. "That's true. Tio cares very much and will find answers. He doesn't want to see another family go through what the Gilley's are experiencing."

Gabi wiggled out of her mother's embrace. "Come on, Lex, let's go say hi to Abuela and see what kind of trouble Abuelo got into today. I'm making dinner tonight, Poppy, are you staying?"

I stood to give her a hug. "I can't tonight, but I would love to do that very soon. I miss you guys."

Lexi hoisted her backpack onto her shoulder. "Just make sure it is a night that Gabi is cooking, and not Tio."

After the girls left the room, I made sure Kim was settled

and walked to the door. Hand on the doorknob, I stopped and turned back to Kim. "How long has Larissa been out of jail?"

Kim waved another page. "That was the last page. She never went. Her attorney convinced the DA that she was so pampered by her parents, she had no concept of right or wrong. They pled down to DUIA—$500 fine, sixty-day license suspension, and a month in a private rehab."

I PULLED into the small parking lot and stared at the red brick building. I could see some resemblance to the photos on the website, but this building seemed much smaller, more modest. Nevertheless, the large sign "First Family Free Fellowship of Texas" stood loud and proud, directing people to the yellow striped asphalt lot. I circled the building until I found a small collection of church vans and a sand-colored Lincoln Continental, which was in the space marked "Pastor Jones."

What is the protocol for entering a church during off-hours? I didn't see any evidence of a doorbell or camera, so I decided on a one-two approach. I knocked on the door, then opened it just enough to stick my head in and call, "Hello?" Greeted by silence, I slipped the rest of my body in, the door closing behind me. "Hello… anyone here?" I heard a vacuum buzzing in the distance, so I followed the sound. At least, I told myself it was a vacuum and not a method of disposing of nosy chefs who wandered in off the highway.

The woman jumped when she saw me. "Good grief! Hal! HAL!!" She stepped backward, placing the vacuum between us. A man stepped from a nearby office, his tie loose and shirt sleeves rolled up, but still clearly a pastor.

"It's okay, Belinda," he placed a large hand on the woman's shoulder. "I'm sure this Sister didn't mean to frighten you. Why don't you stop for the day? Get home and see those grandkids." Belinda muttered and rolled the vacuum away, and I could tell she did not forgive me for my trespasses.

"Pastor Harold Jones," he said as he extended his hand to shake. "What brings you to First Family Free Fellowship today, miss?" I suddenly felt very ill at ease as I realized I was now alone with a strange man, who may have information on a murdered girl, and no one had any idea where I was. "Oh, forgive me!" He stuck his head in the office from where he'd emerged. "Lori, please call Mother to the counseling room." I heard a voice respond, and the squeak of an intercom as it clicked to life.

A moment later, the woman from the photo on the website appeared, her long hair pinned in elaborate loops on her head. I could describe her age as "indeterminate." Although streaks of gray highlighted her long hair, her face was unlined. But her eyes—her eyes were those of a woman who had lived a long life, with lots of stories, lots of pain. Without a word, she unlocked a door down the corridor and held it open. A smile spread across her face. "Welcome to First Family Free Fellowship of Texas, please come in."

The room appeared to be a police interrogation room decorated in 80s Gunne Sax and Laura Ashley. The smell of potpourri was overwhelming, with several bowls scattered about the room, along with a multitude of floral patterns. The couch, a print on the wall, throw pillows in the leather chair that was clearly reserved for the pastor. Yet there was an undercurrent of utilitarianism to the room that the warmth of the frou-frou decorating could not cut through.

"I won't take much of your time," I didn't want to stay a moment longer than necessary. "I'm looking for a friend of your daughter, Cas—"

"Casey!" The woman leapt from her chair. "You know where Casey is?"

Her outburst earned her a sharp look from her husband. "Now, Mother, let's listen to what this young lady has to say." He turned toward me, a pained smile on his face. "Do you, perhaps, attend school with our Cassandra?"

"Cassandra? No," I shook my head. "I'm looking for Casey... I believe they know Larissa Fielding, who was the roommate of my employee. They might be able to help me find out more information about Sarah."

"I'm afraid we are not in the business of investigating individuals, miss." The pastor rose from his chair, his dismissal clear.

"Please!" I could hear the desperation in my voice, but I was running out of options. "Maybe you know her?" I pulled my phone out and flashed the picture of Sarah, a triumphant smile on her face.

I WAS no longer talking to my lifelong friend, Andy Gomez. I was speaking with, rather being spoken *to* by DPS Trooper Andrew Luis Gomez. I'd had the entire drive from Waco to Baseless, his state-issued sedan following close behind, to think about what I'd say. Turns out, that was a waste of time, as it didn't appear he was going to let me speak.

"What in the world were you thinking, Poppy?" He gesticulated wildly as he spoke. "I'll tell you what—you weren't thinking. At all. First of all, you broke into a car that was evidence—"

"I di—"

"You withheld evidence that could have helped us locate Sarah's true identity sooner. You visited—without letting anyone know where you were going—a known drug house. You—"

"But—"

"You took off on an ill-conceived adventure to find

someone called Casey, with no idea of who they were, stepping in the doors of a wannabe-cult, again without letting anyone know where—"

"I found her!" I shouted. "I found Casey, and I found Sarah's parents."

"What you did," he stopped pacing. "Was jeopardize our investigation, place yourself in harm's way, and shock the parents of a murder victim."

My bravado evaporated. "I didn't know she was Sarah."

Trooper Gomez left and my friend Andy returned, his voice and posture softening. "I know, Poppy, but that's why you should've told me what was going on. If I had entered *Casey's* name in our state database, I would have been able to put the pieces together. Even the picture from when she was fifteen—there is no doubt that Casey is Sarah."

I massaged my pounding temples. "Why was she hiding?"

"Her story isn't mine to tell, but I can tell you that kids don't spend seven years in the foster system because things are great at home." He sighed. "Once her parents started their 'church,' they wanted her to be part of it. She didn't, so she ran. When they couldn't find her, they found Larissa. They knew Casey wouldn't be far away, so they sent the letter you found. Or rather, the envelope you found. We still haven't found the letter."

"I'm sorry." I looked up at Andy, tears clouding my vision. I knew I was sorry, but I wasn't sure it was related to my failed investigative attempts, or the deeper knowledge of Sarah's rotten life.

7

I was loading in supplies for the week when I saw the Lincoln pull into the lot. The safety of the taproom seemed miles away at that moment, even though the space between us was full of people enjoying the afternoon sunshine. I thought it might be a bit too obvious if I sprinted for cover, so I waited for the inevitable.

"Miss Price," the pastor's voice was deep and rich, "may we have a moment of your time?"

I looked up, drinking in the sadness in their eyes. It sounds trite, but they look like they'd aged a decade since that day at the church. "I'm so sorry," I choked out the words. "I didn't know. I never would—"

"It's okay," Sarah's mother clasped my arm with both of her hands, her head bowed. "You brought our Casey back to us." She whispered a prayer under her breath, her body swaying as kept a firm grip on me. "It wasn't how we expected, but you brought her back, and we are thankful for that."

I nodded weakly.

"Is this," the pastor waved expansively, "where she worked? Does this all belong to you?"

"Oh, no," I said, leading them to a shaded table, "the taproom belongs to the Martin family. The food truck is mine. That's where Sar- *Casey* worked. She had such talent."

"So, I hear," he nodded. "Is your food truck popular? Do a lot of business?"

I smiled, despite the grim situation. "Yes, after a rough start, it's doing well. Our weekend specials draw people from miles around." I heard my voice pitch higher, my speed increase, as always happened when I started talking about plans for the truck. "Your daughter was a natural when it came to recipe creation. We were already talking about expanding to weekday evening grab and go meals—"

He twisted his mouth into something between a smile and a grimace. "Then why'd you let her get murdered on your watch?"

His question took the breath out of me. "I... I didn't. I mean, she was opening up, and I was on my way. I didn't... I wouldn't..."

Mrs. Jones patted my arm. "It's okay, dear. How could you know that someone would try to rob you that morning? You'd never been robbed before, had you?"

"Never! And it wasn't a robbery—nothing was missing."

"Oh?" They both tilted their heads at the pastor's words. "How very odd and fortuitous for you. A rising star eliminated and not even a shaker of salt missing from your business."

I remained seated, speechless, as they stood and strolled across the parking lot. Easing into their car, they turned to wave, Mrs. Jones calling out to me. "Bless you dear, we will be in touch!

Kim's eyes widened as I told her the story. "That was a threat, Poppy! How could that not be a threat?"

"I don't know," I dropped my head into my hands. "It was surreal. I thought they would be proud of what Sarah was doing, that it would bring them peace to know she was doing well, but instead... I don't know, they just—"

"You need to tell Andy."

"Tell me what?" Andy appeared through the kitchen door, munching an apple.

Kim twisted in her chair to see her brother. "You've got to stop doing that! I'm going to have a heart attack before my leg ever heals. Use. The. Front. Door."

He carefully hung his hat from the coatrack. "It's not like I'm an intruder. I was in the back garden with Mami and decided I'd say hello to you before leaving. So, *hola, mi hermana*. Now, tell me what?"

We both stared for a moment as Andy continued to crunch away on the apple. Finally, Kim broke the silence. "Sarah's parents threatened Poppy."

"No," I jumped into the conversation. "They didn't really threaten me... more like accused me."

"Accused you of what, exactly?"

"There is no 'exactly' to it. It was all very roundabout, but I think they believe I have something to do with Sarah's death."

"Casey... Cassandra," Andy corrected.

"Or Molly," Kim piped up.

"It doesn't matter what we call her, I didn't kill her! For Pete's sake, I'm trying to figure out who did kill her."

"Whoa," Andy held both palms toward me. "Back it up there. You are not doing anything of the such. I thought we cleared this up after your trip to Waco? I investigate, you chef."

Kim rolled her eyes. "Chef isn't a verb."

He waved her off. "The fact remains that you," he pointed to me, "and you," and at Kim, "are not investigating anything. You need to stay out of the whole affair and should something land in your lap that might be important, you need to turn it over immediately. And," he stood to carry his core to the compost bowl. "let's not forget that Poppy has not been officially cleared as a suspect."

We both erupted in shouts of disagreement. "They let me go!" "She didn't do it!"

Andy plucked his hat from the coatrack. "I know Poppy didn't do it, but Baseless PD is not going to officially clear anyone until they make an arrest. A real arrest." He moved to the front door. "Seriously, Poppy, stay away from the Pastor and Mother. I get a bad vibe from them."

The door closed and Kim immediately started muttering under her breath and it quickly escalated. "… little boy couldn't even wipe his own—"

"Kim!"

"I'm sorry, I just get so frustrated with his high and mighty attitude! I'm not some frat boy caught speeding on the interstate, I practically rais—"

"Kim!" I waved my arms to catch her attention. "He's just doing his job. And, anyway, I'm the one that got the brunt of it. I don't think he believes you are sneaking out at night to investigate."

She adjusted the throw blanket covering her leg. "No, I'm not going anywhere." A cat-like smile crept across her face. "But people come to me."

I was equal parts curious and afraid. "Who?"

"Mami and Papi have home health that come in, I'm getting PT three times a week, Ellie from down the street picks up our groceries once a week and puts them up. Oh, and the girls have friends—"

"Okay, I get it. Grand Central. Cut to the chase."

"Wednesday PT is Keri, a sweet young lady, just a couple of years older than you. Do you know her? I think she played bask—"

"Kim!"

"Okay, her mother is Rose, who happens to be—"

"The receptionist at the police department!"

Kim wrinkled her nose at my interruption. "I believe she is the Office Manager. Anyway, she is privy to a lot of confidential information and she loves to come home and chat about it. And Keri said she's pretty sure it is okay to talk about it with her patients because of doctor-patient confidentiality."

"Is she a doctor? Is that how that works? I don't think that's how it works."

"She is not a doctor, and that is not how it works. But did you want me to tell her that, or did you want me to find out who they are investigating?" I clamped my mouth closed and waited. "That's what I thought. The Pastor and Mother lost Casey to Child Protective Services when she was eleven-years-old. She told a teacher that her parents were abusing her." I gasped. "Not like that! Making her stand at the wall for an hour if she didn't clean her plate, stuff like that. Even though their disciplinary techniques were not what you might call progressive, Casey was healthy, well-fed, and safe, so there was no reason to remove her, or her two siblings. Shortly after the first investigation, Casey ran away. She was returned home, and they ordered them to attend family counseling. They did, then Casey started self-harming. She would run away repeatedly, and she would always say she ran away because her parents said cruel things to her."

"What did her siblings say?"

"Nothing! They were just preschoolers, and they seemed perfectly happy and adjusted. Of course, the parents denied it all. It went back and forth like that for a bit until they placed her in a psych unit. It was the opinion of the doctors that Casey was telling the truth, so they placed her back in foster care. That started a whole roller coaster—the parents would complete parenting classes, she'd be returned, and she'd start acting out again, and back to another foster family. She had nine placements in seven years, plus her stint in the hospital."

"Oh, my gosh," a lump formed in my throat. "No wonder she wanted to change her name and get away. What happened to the other kids?"

"They never had any problem. No cries of abuse. The parents passed every evaluation with flying colors." Kim twisted the fringe of her lap blanket in her nervous hands. "You know what that means? Either they really didn't do anything wrong, and Casey was lying all that time, or Casey was telling the truth, and they were able to fool everyone into thinking she was the problem. I'm afraid it is the latter, and that scares me."

"How did they find her?" I ducked my head in embarrassment. "I mean, other than me."

"Larissa," Kim said simply. "Larissa and Casey met in junior high, and even when Casey moved to her next foster placement, her next school, they stayed fast friends. Larissa wasn't trying to hide, so all they had to do was find her and wait. They knew that eventually their daughter would be there too."

I DOODLED the numbers over and over, moving them around, looking for an answer. 76432. I researched obscure numerology texts, and Lexi's junior code breaker book, hoping to find anything to help me find the meaning behind the numbers tucked away in Sarah's glove box.

The afternoon sun fell in just the right way across the sofa, and I was just drifting into a much-needed nap when a scene played behind my eyelids, forcing me into wakefulness.

THE CORRIDORS WERE EMPTY, but I knew it would only be a matter of time before they would fill with people, mostly students, returning from their day. The window for testing my hypothesis was closing.

I knocked vigorously and placed my ear on the door, listening for any sign of activity inside. Hearing none, I quickly tapped 76432 on the keypad. The indicator light turned green, and the bolt clicked open. I slipped inside, gently closing the door behind me.

Larissa was not much of a housekeeper which might explain why she seemed so intent on keeping me in the corridor on my last visit. I crossed the small living room to search for bedrooms, hoping a peek at Sarah's room might hold some huge clue, overlooked by the PD and DPS. Instead, I found a police seal across the door. *In for a penny, in for a pound.* I carefully lifted the tape with the edge of my nail, cursing that I hadn't brought my bag, which always had kitchen gloves.

Sarah's room was much different from the rest of the apartment. Sparsely decorated, and neat, it could have come straight out of the Ikea catalog. It probably did come straight out of the Ikea catalog. The bookshelf was lined with cook-books, books on cooking techniques, and memoirs by chefs of all stripes. I found no fiction and very few personal items. Slipped in between *The Flavor Bible* and *Kitchen Confidential*, stood a thin volume with gold lettering on the spine. *Redemption Academy Yearbook* A silk ribbon marked a page dedicated to the 7th grade girls' choir. A heart drawn in purple ink framed two smiling girls, and curly script proclaimed them "sisters." Even though I had no doubt, I checked the caption, Larissa Fielding and Cassandra Jones.

Aware that the clock was ticking, I slipped down the hall to the next bedroom. I stumbled on a pair of red-soled shoes that cost more than my house payment and kicked them into a pile of dirty clothes. I didn't worry that Larissa would be able to tell that someone had been in her room. I moved quickly, opening and closing drawers, perhaps looking for a handwritten confession, as that seemed to be the only thing that could solve this mystery. Third drawer down, right-hand side. It was a little sticky, so I almost didn't hear the five beeps and sound of the lock sliding open. I hurriedly closed the door and crept back to Sarah's room.

My heart pounded at the sound of Larissa's voice. "Just give me five minutes to change, okay? Kaleb is hot; I want to look good." There was a mumbled response from the direction of the living room. "Sure, go ahead and cut it. A little bump won't hurt." A door slammed closed. "I couldn't find my shoes!" More mumbled voices, some high-pitched laughter. After an interminable time, the front door closed, and the apartment fell silent. I counted to one hundred, then scurried to the front door where I prayed that there would be no one in the corridor.

Covered in a cold sweat, I slipped behind the wheel of my car. I was sure that everyone in the busy parking lot was looking at me, and every brunette I spotted morphed into Larissa. I pulled on to the main road and hit the interstate, no destination in mind. I just needed to get far away from that apartment as soon as possible while I pondered how a drawer full of cash might play into murder.

8

I placed the morning's receipts into the bank bag, then turned to Jake. "How well do you know Larissa?"

"Ris? I don't know…. moderately well. Why?"

"I just…" I debated whether or not to tell him about my excursion to the apartment. "She and Sarah were obviously very close. I guess I'm just trying to emotionally close the book on what happened."

He finished wiping down the counter and shoved the rag into the laundry bag. "Does that mean you don't think they are going to find who killed Sarah?"

"I don't know. Maybe?" To be honest, I didn't know if they were any closer to finding her killer than when I walked up on the scene a week ago. "I thought it would be easier when I found out her real identity, but I think it just complicated everything. I don't know what I'm looking for, but I can't—"

"Looking for? What do you mean *looking for*? I thought that cop told you to stay out of it."

"He did—and I am. Mostly." I shoved the bank bag into the laundry bag and hoisted it over my shoulder. "Now that they've got this overdose to investigate, I don't think Sarah's death is a top priority."

Jake held the door open for me, checking to make sure I flipped the sign to 'closed'. "What is there to investigate? ODs happen."

"They are waiting for final reports, but they think the drugs might have been contaminated. And, even if they weren't, drugs in the high school are a big deal." I secured the lock on the door. "They aren't going to rest until they find out where they came from."

Jake nodded. "I hope you're right. My life would have ended up a lot differently if someone had cut off my source early on."

THEY PACKED the high school gym for Rhys Gilley's memorial service. There wasn't a church in Baseless that was large enough to host the crowd, and unpredictable spring weather made an outdoor service a poor choice. Students, faculty, parents, and community members filled the bleachers, and the chairs placed under the hoops at each end of the floor. A casket covered with a maroon and gold floral spray stood at center court, a somber reminder that this was not a cele-bration.

How are you supposed to eulogize a 16-year-old who lost their life to a stupid mistake? Several people tried—most told stories reinforcing what a good kid he was. Always there for his friends. An altar boy (literally). An honor student and athlete. A son and brother. But they all ended with the ques-tion why. Why did a stellar guy with his whole life in front of him decide that snorting meth was a good way to spend an afternoon? To that question, they had no answers.

I came with Aaron to support Cam, even though the students were kept on the opposite side of the gym. It was still a school day. Aaron's dad, as well as several staff members from the taproom—also considered family—spread throughout the crowd. I poked a finger in Aaron's shoulder as we stood for another hymn and hissed, "Look! What is she doing here?"

Aaron faced me with a scowl. "Stop that! What's your problem?"

"Over there!" I dipped my head toward the chairs under the home net. "It's Larissa—Sarah's roommate."

"She's sitting by the family."

"Why? She's not family!"

Aaron stared straight ahead, singing weakly with the crowd. He was done talking.

The service ended with a prayer and a shout of "Go, Squirrels!" from the students. Pep rally or memorial service, you never leave the gym without a shout to support your team. Thankfully, they wheeled the still-closed casket out before dismissing the crowd. Emotion was thick in the gym and I could not imagine what it would be like if several hundred people—half of them teens—had to file by and say their last goodbyes. Even several of the crying-is-for-sissies dads had tears in their eyes, I'm sure from the thought that it just as easily could have been their child.

I spotted Larissa again as we filed out into the sunlight. I snaked through the crowd and came up on her side. "Oh, Larissa!" I tried to look surprised, but the look on her face said I might not have pulled it off. "I didn't know you knew Rhys."

She pulled her sunglasses from her purse, along with a piece of gum she popped into her mouth. "Erin is Chi Sigma Zeta. I came for her." It was then that I realized I was deep in a group of twenty-something females all wearing the same color blue dress and heels, matching Chi Sigma Zeta necklaces draped across their uniformly thin and tan necks. "We support all our sisters, even the OG."

It was then that I realized Erin must be Mrs. Gilley. "Oh, so you didn't actually know Rhys?"

She sniffed. "I'd met him. The little kids are always trying to hang out at parties, but we send them away."

"Parties?"

"Um, yes, those things that people with lives go to. Music, booze, friends?" She looked me up and down disdainfully. "But I can see why you wouldn't be familiar."

Ouch. I was just about to launch into my speech about how my life of hard work was rewarding when Aaron's hand touched my shoulder. "Come on, Pops, let's get out of here. I need to get back to the taproom." Larissa gave him a lecherous smile, but he didn't see it, he was already on his way to the car.

I smiled at her. "I'll see you later?"

"Whatever." She melted back into the strum of blue-clad Barbies and disappeared.

9

I spotted Pastor at the end of the breakfast rush. Today he was missing his suit jacket and had sleeves rolled up to his elbows, but he was still every bit a southern preacher. He made his way to the window and ordered a cup of coffee. "Miss Price, we are having a funeral service for our Cassandra and would like to invite you to attend."

My mind flashed back to the last encounter with Pastor and Mother. His entire demeanor was completely different, and the threatening aura was gone. Andy's warning echoing in my mind, I blurted out, "Do you have a minute? Could we sit down and talk?"

The lines around his eyes crinkled as a genuine smile spread across his face. "Thank you, I'd like that very much."

I left Jake in charge and led Mr. Jones to the same table where we'd sat with his wife. The same table where questions had turned to accusations. I wasted no time in getting to the point. "Why do you want me to attend the memorial? The last time we spoke, you all but accused me of being involved in your daughter's death."

He dropped his head with a sigh, gripping the disposable coffee cup like a lifeline. After a long moment, he returned his gaze to mine. "I'm sorry. You must understand… life with Cassandra was difficult. She often found herself involved with—unsavory characters, I suppose is the best description. We were afraid that she had, once again, latched on to the wrong person and landed in trouble. It wasn't about you; it was about the people from her past."

"Like Larissa?"

Something flashed in his eyes. "Yes, Larissa. We easily could have lost Cassandra a dozen times over when she was with Larissa. I'm sure you know about the wreck that killed that poor man—"

"He died? The article said—"

Pastor held up a hand to stop my confused rambling. "They grievously injured him in the accident. He spent over three years in misery before he finally succumbed two weeks ago."

"His poor family."

"Yes, indeed, they are rightfully angry that they had a son, husband, and father snatched from them, yet no justice served. There were other, less newsworthy wrecks. A trip to the ER with alcohol poisoning. Expulsion from school for having drugs on her person. Oh, and the weekend they ran away to Denver to meet with an older man they had met on the internet." He smiled weakly. "And that is just the surface of what Larissa involved Cassandra in."

My mind swirled as I tried to reconcile what he was telling me with the Sarah that I knew. Perhaps that was the secret–he spoke of Cassandra and I knew Sarah. "Why did you allow her friendship with Larissa to continue?"

He laughed at my question. "It wasn't our choice. You could count on one hand the number of months Cassandra was in our care after she met Larissa. We'd already been having problems with Casey making baseless claims, running away and the like, for about two years. We knew the teen years could be a problem, so we scrimped and saved and enrolled her in Redemption Academy. We thought we were doing the best thing for her, but it turned out to be the worst thing we could have done."

"That's where she met Larissa?"

"Yes," he sipped from the cup. "We thought it was a blessing at first. The girls were inseparable, and for a few months, things were better at home. We believed we'd finished with the foster home merry-go-round. Then came the first time Larissa got Cassandra into trouble—they cheated on a test. We punished her, and she called her social worker in tears."

"How," I approached the subject carefully. "Did you punish her? Wasn't that the basis of her abuse claims?"

His eyes flashed with sudden anger. "Well, I see you've done your homework! We never abused Cassandra, or our other two children. Never. If you'd like to read the reports from over the years, you will find that every, single one said there was no sign of abuse in the home. We completed every parenting class with flying colors. Our two youngest children were happy and thriving. But Cassandra, she wanted... I don't know what she wanted, but it wasn't us. And she understood the way to get away from us was to tell the people what they wanted to hear—that we were abusive."

"I didn't mean to insult you." My eyes drifted to the food truck, reassuring myself that Jake was within shouting distance. "I'm just trying to wrap my mind around all of this. The girl I knew as Sarah—your Cassandra—was completely unlike what you are describing to me. She was quiet and kind and completely driven to become a chef."

"It's good to know that somewhere along the way, her drive shifted to something more productive."

"When was the last time you saw her?"

"Not too long after the accident. She was 16 or so and it was clear that she had no use for us. She actually said the words, 'I don't want you in my life.' So, we let her go." My sharp intake of breath at that revelation made him pause. "Not completely, mind you. We still sent her letters, pictures of her siblings. We made sure she understood we were standing by if she ever changed her mind. But the endless loop of social service workers, the bouncing from a foster to us and back, we put an end to that."

"I'm so sorry." My heart raced as I pondered what might cause a 16-year-old to reject their family in that way. "Why did you try to find her? I mean, now, when you'd already given her up?"

"We'd always hoped that she'd come around once she matured." He leaned in, conspiratorially. "You know a brain doesn't even finish developing until sometime in a person's twenties? We thought she needed to grow, mature, and discover what life was really like after leaving the foster care system. We probably should have waited, but we needed to bring her home for the church."

"The church?"

"The church is just about to launch a parenting course. I guess we got something out of all those classes." He chuckled. "We first taught locally, in small groups, but the demand seemed to be bigger. We've invested a lot of time and money in setting up the course to launch online—churches all over the world can follow our plan for raising their children."

"It doesn't look great to have a parenting course when your own child was taken awa—"

"Don't you think we know that? It was fine until some nosy parker in Waco heard about Cassandra from their cousin in Lubbock. They started raising a stink, and it even caused our members to have doubts—attendance dropped in half in the weeks after they started gabbing."

"So, you told people she was at college."

"Of course! What else could we do? We couldn't let her restless and rebellious spirit ruin everything. We let people know she was studying and would be home soon—and we set about trying to find her. We knew she'd be with Larissa, so once we'd found her, we just waited." I sat quietly as he stared into the distance, his mind somewhere else. "We offered her money. That's what was in the letter—we'd give her a share of the parenting course money if she would just show up and let people see that, despite the turmoil of the early years, she respected us as parents. That's what it is all about, you know, training a child to respect you. They can't grow into good people without respect and obedience."

His last words shook me. "She still didn't want to be part of your family, she wasn't *obedient*." The word left a sour taste in my mouth.

"No, despite our best efforts, obedience was not in Cassandra's vocabulary. Her mutiny almost cost us everything…"

"Almost? Now you have no way to mend your relationship, no way to prove you are good parents."

"We no longer have to. They took our daughter from us in an act of senseless violence because we did not teach her respect and obedience when she was young. We learned our lessons from her, and we can teach other parents how to avoid the same grim outcome."

"Hey, Poppy!" Jake waved from the door of the truck. "I could use a little help when you've got a minute."

"Be right there!" I jumped from the table, glad for an excuse to leave the uncomfortable discussion. "Thank you for stopping by, but I've got to get back to work."

"Of course, of course. Saturday morning at 11:00, at the First Family Free Fellowship sanctuary. We will sit in vigil for the twelve-hours prior. We are sending our Cassandra off in grand style—you don't want to miss it."

As I hurried back to the truck, I couldn't help but think he sounded more like a man planning the grand opening of a car lot than a man mourning the death of his long-lost child.

I POPPED INTO THE TRUCK, ready to work, only to find Jake tapping away on his phone. "I thought you needed help!"

"Well…" he peeked out the door at Pastor. "I thought you might need help. The conversation looked intense. You can always go back and tell him I couldn't figure out how to change the register tape."

"You're right, it was intense. I think I'll just stay here and wait for the lunch crowd. He makes me a little—"

"Unsettled?" Jake queried.

"Yes, that's the word, unsettled! I don't know what it is about him, and his wife, for that matter. The first time I met them, they practically accused me of being involved in Sarah's death. This time he told me what a horrible kid she was and was practically giddy talking about the memorial plans. I know people grieve differently, but this…. it gives me the heebie-jeebies."

"The Pastor and Mother are a weird couple, to be sure."

"You know them?"

Jake looked uncomfortable. "I've met them. They came by to have a shouting match with Ris, and I was there."

"Really? They had an argument with Larissa?"

"No, not really an argument, it was just the three of them shouting at each other. They accused Ris of keeping Sarah away from them; Ris accused them of being bad parents. It wasn't anything that hadn't been said before, it was just said much more loudly. I finally got them to calm down and leave when I pointed out that if the cops showed up, so would local media."

I laughed. "You mean Hank? Sarah's murder was on page two of the weekly paper, a ribbon-cutting at the new gym was page one. I don't think he's listening to the police scanner for leads."

He smiled. "I wasn't even sure if there was any local

media in Baseless, but I was sure that they wouldn't be happy with any bad press. According to Ris, he's trying to grow that place into a mega-church, so he'll rake in the mega-bucks. He never cared about Sarah, he just cared about what she could do for him."

"I guess you and Larissa didn't get invited to the memorial service then?"

"Not a chance. They don't want anyone who knew Cassandra to be there."

"Cassandra? You didn't know her as Cassan—"

"I didn't know her when she was Cassandra, but I knew it was her real name. She and Ris used to talk about it, and they showed me a yearbook from when they went to school together."

"Choir."

"How did you know?"

I momentarily thought about telling him the truth. "Her dad mentioned it today... Redemption Academy. They were in choir together. Why... why didn't you tell me this earlier? You knew I was trying to find out Sarah's true identity."

His gaze drifted to the floor. "I thought I was protecting her. Cassandra didn't exist anymore. Molly didn't exist anymore. She had worked so hard to become Sarah, to be someone without a past, reaching for her dreams. I couldn't save her, but I thought I could at least protect her memory."

I thought about his reasoning. Would I have done differently in his situation? She had entrusted him with a secret, but the trust didn't die with her. "I understand... I think. But they need that information to find out who killed her."

"Do they? They know who she was, they know all about her family, and the foster homes. I still don't see anyone in jail. The only thing that accomplished is that now people around here will remember her for the messed-up kid she was, not Sarah."

I spied our first lunch customer crunching across the gravel lot. "Do you think it could have been her dad?"

"Yes," he said as he opened the order window, "and if it was, he'll get away with it, just like he got away with what he did all those years ago."

10

I yawned as I made my way toward the food truck. I should have stayed late yesterday, but my conversation with Sarah's dad had left me feeling like I needed a shower and a nap. That was all well and good for yesterday's Poppy, but that meant today's Poppy had to start work while most of Baseless was still deep in REM sleep.

"My dear Sarah..." The words drifted on the early morning fog. I could have convinced myself it was my imagination until I heard a hiccupping sob. I followed the sound and crept silently to the front of the truck where I spied a figure crouched on the damp ground, a bouquet clutched in his hands. I reached for my phone, not knowing who to call, but sure this was not a situation I wanted to be involved in.

"Hello?" The man's head jerked up as he peered into the gray morning. "Is someone there?" His voice held a tremor, but I wasn't sure if it was from fear or age. He attempted to rise, but stumbled, falling face first to the ground with a shocked cry.

Instincts kicked in and I ran to his side. The memory that infamous serial killer Ted Bundy would feign an injury to lure victims to him passed through my mind as I dropped to the ground beside the man. "Let me help you—" Danger be damned, a Texas girl is raised to help a neighbor. I no more could have ignored his cries of pain than I could have flown across the parking lot by flapping my arms.

The man rolled over with a moan. "I'm fine. I just wanted to remember dear Sarah. I didn't think anyone would be here and you—"

Righteous anger ripped through me. "It's my food truck— why in the world wouldn't I be here!"

The man closed his eyes as if he had given up on life and was ready to die on the damp grass. "Because it is three o'clock in the morning."

"Oh," my anger drained away. "That's fair." Blood dripped from a cut in the man's forehead. "Come on," I grabbed his hands and attempted to pull him from the ground. "Let's get that cut cleaned up." If he was feigning injury to nab a victim, he was doing an excellent job.

He continued to moan and groan as he rose from the ground. We stood eye to eye, making him all of 5 foot 5 inches tall. He was slim, but soft. I had arms like a longshore-man, thanks to hauling boxes from the walk-in at the brew-ery, up the hill to the truck. His gait was unstable, and I felt sure that if it came to a physical altercation, I could easily overcome him. I pushed further thoughts of it being a ruse out of my mind as I unlocked the door and led him to a seat inside the food truck. My kitchen knives gleamed from their spot on the wall, a mere five feet from where he sat. They were a beautiful, matched set, except for a new ebony-handled, twelve-inch chef's knife. It was a replacement for my Wüsthof. The one that someone had shoved through Sarah's liver, causing her to bleed to death in under five minutes.

I dabbed a wet cloth around the cut, trying to determine the extent of his wound. "Since I'm fixing you up, I feel like I have the right to know who you are and what you are doing outside of my business in the wee hours of the morning." He nodded, and I hissed at him. "Hold still!"

"Yes," he sighed. "Thank you for helping."

We sat silently for a moment before I pressed on. "I am still waiting for answers."

"Of course," his voice was soft, and had lost the tremor from outside. "I'm William Wrigley. I was leaving flowers for poor, sweet Sarah." His voice hitched with emotion at Sarah's name.

"How do you know Sarah and why haven't I ever seen you before?"

"Oh, my dear," he almost laughed. "You have! I am the invisible man—it is both a blessing and a curse. I am the most forgettable, blend into the background, no-I-don't-think-I've-seen-him man around. There is nothing extraordinary about me, not even an unsightly wart on my nose that would at least make people notice me."

"I'm sure I would have remembered. I'm known for the food I serve, but I make a point to remember people. People like to be remembered—they aren't remembered because they are regulars, they are regulars because they are remembered."

"That may be true, but to be remembered, one first must be seen."

I thought about his words and wondered if it was truly possible that there were people who I didn't see, but they just blended into the background noise. "So, Mr. Invisible Man William Wrigley, why did you choose to remember Sarah at three in the morning, and how did you know her?"

He winced as I touched an antiseptic wipe to the cut. "I met Sarah when she was working at St. Andrew's. She was such a delightful girl, and she *saw* me. The last time I saw her was last week when I came here for a cup of coffee and instead found her covered with a sheet and police tape around the entire area. I wanted to pay my respects here, quietly, and replace that image with something nicer."

I peered in to the first aid kit, looking for a butterfly bandage. "Your cut isn't too deep, but it's rather long and wide. It really needs a butterfly bandage, or maybe even a couple of stitches. I can't help with either of those. I've got some bandages, although there is a choice of brown or JoJo Siwa, and neither of those can keep you from having a scar."

"A scar? How long is the cut?"

"Eh, about two inches? It's ugly, but not deep, so it should heal up just fine."

He nodded slowly. "You are saying that if we merely apply a plain bandage, I may end up with a two-inch long scar on my forehead."

"Yes," I snapped the first aid kit closed.

He reached out and touched my arm. "I'll take the JoJo Siwa, please."

"COULD you run over to the pharmacy and pick up a few things for me please?"

Jake wiped his hands on the dishtowel and took the list from me. "Um, sure. Am I picking up the secret ingredient that keeps the bar crowds coming on the weekends?"

"Ha! Not quite. I had to use the first aid kit this morning, and I noticed it is missing a lot. Just take this list—"

"What happened?" Jake seemed genuinely concerned. "Why did you need the first aid kit?"

I waved away his concern. "It was no big deal. William Wrigley stumbled out front and—"

"William Wrigley?" Anger flashed across Jake's face. "What was he doing here?"

"You know him?"

"Yes, I know him, he was stalking Sarah. That creep needs to stay away from here."

The accusation from Jake rolled around my brain with the

events of this morning. I had decided that William Wrigley was a harmless, older man who was lonely and found a kind spirit in Sarah. What if I was wrong, and he *was* stalking her? "He seemed nice; I can't believe he was stalking her."

"Oh, believe it. Every night at the taproom. Then he started showing up here. I told him to stay away, to leave Sarah alone."

"Lots of people have a favorite waitress, or—"

"He's a stalker." Jake stopped on his way out the door. "I'm telling you, Poppy, you do not want to get involved with William Wrigley. His Mr. Invisible Man schtick is just a way to get you to put down your guard."

The door closed behind Jake and I thought about what he's said as I finished cleaning up from the day. William had seemed so sincere in his fondness for Sarah, and his grief. It is possible that he mistook her kindness for a deeper interest in him. It's also possible that Jake mistook William's awkwardness for something else. It could all be a big misunderstanding. Or it could be the lead to finally finding Sarah's murderer.

Kim HELD her phone away from her ear, and I could clearly hear the frustration in Andy's voice. "I told the two of you to stop investigating!"

"We're not investigating!" Kim shouted into the phone at her brother. "Hang on, I'm putting you on speaker so Poppy can explain."

"Poppy, I hate to do this, but as a duly appointed—"

"I KNOW!" I cut Andy off before he could finish his oft-repeated speech about being a duly appointed officer of the law, blah, blah, blah… "I wasn't investigating anything. I had to go in early and he was there leaving flowers where Sarah died. I don't know which one of us was more frightened by the other. He seemed perfectly harmless, but then Jake told me that William had been stalking Sarah."

"He told us that, too."

Kim and I talked over each other. "Is he a stalker?" "He's a stalker!" "Is he dangerous?" "Another suspect!"

"Stop!" Even though I couldn't see Andy, I could imagine him pinching the bridge of his nose, eyes closed, as he tried to reset his brain. "We checked him out, and he seems perfectly harmless. He walked up on the scene not long after you, Poppy."

Kim blurted out. "But murderers sometimes return to the scene of the crime! He could have been coming by to see his handiwork."

"That's true, but if that is our criteria for making someone a suspect, there are at least two dozen of Poppy's regular customers who need to be hauled in for questioning. He's a lonely man who had a favorite waitress. He has no past record of violence. No complaints against him. And the allegations of stalking came from Jake, not Sarah. It is more likely that Jake's just a jealous boyfriend."

I flopped against the couch cushions. "Do I need to worry about William Wrigley?"

"No."

"Do I need to worry about Pastor and Mother?"

There was a long pause before he answered. "I'm not sure."

Kim tried to leap from her chair and was rudely reminded of her broken leg. "I knew it! They killed Sarah so that they could move on with their crazy parenting course. He as much as admitted it to Poppy!"

"Kim!" I gave her a look to remind her that Andy didn't know about my latest conversation with Pastor.

"Poppy." Andy's voice was steady.

"Yes...."

"I need you to come over to the station. Now."

BASED on the tone of voice used when Andy not-so-kindly requested my presence, it thrilled me that he did not meet me with a pair of handcuffs. He led me down the hall, past his office, and opened the door to an interrogation room. I stopped in the doorway and turned back to him; a questioning look on my face.

"Take a seat, please." He motioned to the hard plastic chairs. "We'll be with you in just a minute. Could I bring you a drink?"

Maybe I watch too much television, but I thought back to a pair of hardened New York City detectives providing a suspect with drink after drink until his bladder was full, then refusing to let him use the facilities. Intense questioning with a full bladder was more than he could take, and he confessed to a crime he didn't commit in order to be taken to the men's room. I swallowed, my mouth dry, "No, thank you."

He returned with his partner, Trooper Walter Moore. I didn't have to wonder long about who was going to play good cop and who was going to play bad cop. Trooper Moore dropped a folder in front of me and Andy quickly closed it. "Hang on, Walt, let's talk to her about why she's here before you start the shock and awe campaign."

"This," Trooper Moore rapped his knuckles on the folder. "is why she's here. We have a dangerous killer on the loose and she and your sister are out playing *Charlie's Angels*."

"There were three of them." The look from Andy told me this was not the time for showing off my trivia skills. "And we're not playing anything. We can't help it if information comes our way—you should be glad for our help!"

"You're not helping! You're interfering with an investigation."

"Slow down for a minute." Andy turned from his partner to me. "You are here as a material witness in the murder investigation of Cassandra Jones, known to you as Sarah Brown. You do not have to speak to us, but we may seek a court order to have you involuntarily deposed of information. You are not under arrest and are not a suspect in this case."

I crossed my arms against the chill in the room. "You said I was a suspect."

"No, I said that the Baseless PD considers you a suspect. And quite a few people in Baseless may consider you a suspect. But investigators with the Texas Department of Public Safety do not consider you a suspect in this murder case."

I didn't like the way he parsed his reply. "In this case? Am I a suspect in some other case?"

"Yes," Trooper Moore leaned menacingly across the table. "You are the prime suspect in an obstruction of justice case for interference in a murder investigation. Your meddling is messing up our investigation and putting you at risk. We've got people breathing down our necks to get this thing solved, and you are practically waving a red flag at the killer. The last thing we need is two dead girls."

I looked at Andy, waiting for him to refute what his partner was saying. To tell me not to meddle. To tell me that Sarah's killer was probably long gone from our little town. To tell me it would all be over soon. He didn't. He just stared at a spot on the wall, refusing to make eye contact with me.

"Okay," I said. "What do you want from me?"

IT TURNS out that they wanted almost four hours of my time. I dug through my purse, looking for coins as I stood in front of the soda machine. My mouth felt like the Sahara and my stomach grumbled.

A hand reached around me and dropped coins into the

machine. "I asked you multiple times if you wanted a drink and you told me no."

I snatched the bottle of cold water from behind the flap and downed most of it in one long drink. "I wasn't thirsty."

Andy laughed. "And I can tell by the roar of your stomach that you also are not hungry." He stepped to the next machine and procured a bag of chips. "I'm still your friend, Poppy."

"It didn't seem like it in that interrogation room. An INTERROGATION ROOM, Andy, like I'm some kind of criminal!"

He glanced at the watch on his wrist. "Look, Walt might be a little heavy handed, but what he said is true. We have a lot of leads, but none of them are solid, so we don't really know what kind of criminal we're looking for. If they are still around, and they think you know something… well, I couldn't live with myself if you got hurt because I didn't do my job. Let me do my job, please."

I let out a long breath. "Okay, do your job."

He punched me lightly on the arm. "Not now. My shift ended ten minutes ago. I need to run home and change—I'll pick you up in an hour and we'll hit the taproom. My treat."

He smiled and batted his eyes in an exaggerated manner, and I realized that even when doing his job, Andy was still my friend. He was still the boy that grew up down the street. Still the one who covered for me when I accidentally broke the church window with a baseball. He was still just Andy.

11

The taproom was unusually crowded for a weekday night. I guess the longer days were drawing people out. I wondered if I should consider opening in the evenings every night for the summer.

"Pops? Pops!" I startled as Aaron tapped his pen on my hand. "You in there?"

"Sorry, yes, I was just thinking—" Aaron and Andy both burst into laughter. "That's an old joke guys, don't you think it is time to give it up?"

"Not at all," Aaron replied. "But I do need your order because it is crazy in here tonight." He motioned down the bar to let a customer know he saw him.

"Surprise me," I said.

"And a large app sampler, please," Andy added, "we're starving."

Aaron exhaled. "That's gonna be about 45 minutes. The kitchen is backed up and I'm the only one working the front." Andy and I looked at each other and stood up from our places at the bar. "Aw, come on, guys!"

Andy held out his hands, fist on a flat palm. "One, two,

three, show me what you got!" He grimaced at the result. "I'll bus tables and run the dishwasher."

I smiled at Aaron. "You want me on the floor or in the kitchen?"

The first thing I did in the kitchen was drop a large batch of fries for me. I could help them get through the rush, but not if I passed out in the fryer. Commercially prepared frozen potatoes cooked in cheap grease never tasted so good. Actually, the food at the taproom wasn't that bad. It wasn't meant to be good—that's why I was there on the weekends—it was meant to keep patrons at their tables.

Andy dropped a bus tub at the dishwasher and then grabbed a handful of my fries. "Aren't you glad I offered to take you out? I could write a book on how to apologize."

I narrowed my eyes at him. "A few suggestions—don't, get your hands off my fries, and get back to work."

I stepped out front to check the size of the crowd. I could see that Andy hadn't hit the patio tables, so I grabbed another tub and headed outside. The crowd was diminishing, but there were a few people waiting for a table where they could smoke. Well, where they could smoke until Aaron came out and reminded them that St. Andrew's is a no-smoking establishment, at which point they would grumble and threaten to go somewhere else. Some people just didn't know, but with other patrons it was a well-established ritual. They must believe that someday Aaron would give in and plop an ashtray down, rather than point across the street and invite them to visit The Tipsy Lady.

I made my way through the thinning crowd and glimpsed a familiar figure out of the corner of my eye. I moved closer, squinting into the deepening shadows. An unfamiliar voice drifted to me. "That's all I've got—"

"You're going to need to do better than that." That voice I recognized. Larissa.

The unfamiliar voice dropped, and I could only make out a few words. "promised" "please" "help"

I stepped closer and called out loudly. "Are you waiting for a table? I've just cleared several." Larissa turned and her eyes narrowed at me. I feigned surprise. "Oh, hey, Ris," The name felt wrong in my mouth, but I thought using the familiar term employed by Jake might endear me to her. "I didn't realize that was you."

"I'm waiting on friends, so I'll stand."

I tried to peer around her and see the person she was with. "Well, two of you are here, so you can grab a table—"

"No, he's not with me." She pointed to a small group coming down the hill. "There's my group now." She glanced over her shoulder at the faceless voice, then back at me, standing her ground between us. I heard another mumble and saw the back of a tall figure loping away.

I snatched the bus tub up and sprinted for the door. "Aaron'll-be-out-to-take-your-order-soon!" The words ran together as I raced to the kitchen. I dropped the tub and pushed open the back door just in time to see the faceless voice reach his companions standing in the dumpster's shadow. I couldn't hear what they were saying, nor could I make out any faces, but I could make out that one of them was wearing a Baseless High school letterman's jacket. The fierce squirrel on the back sneered at me as the group walked away across Pecan Road.

Aaron popped his head into the kitchen. "What's going on, Pops? You ran through like a bat outta hell!"

I returned to pick up the tub of dirty dishes I had discarded. "Sorry, I thought I saw something weird."

Andy peeked from around the dishwasher. "What kind of weird?"

"Larissa—"

"Poppy!" Andy stalked through the kitchen, hands on

hips. "We just discussed this—today—you need to stay away from everyone involved with Sarah."

I immediately became defensive. "She was outside where I was bussing tables—because SOMEONE is slacking on the job!"

Andy opened his mouth to reply, and Aaron stepped between us. "Stop. I appreciate the help, but this isn't helping." Chagrined, the fire went out of us. Wordlessly, I grabbed the next ticket and dumped another batch of fries. I heard Andy mutter something under his breath and then the clink of a tray of glassware being lifted. The door swung as Aaron returned to the front of the house, and it was as if we had stepped back in time by an hour. Order, cook, serve, clean, repeat.

We worked peacefully at a steady pace until the crowd started thinning around ten o'clock. It was the grill cook, Caleb, who kindly suggested I take my leave. "Don't you open your truck at, like, five in the morning?" Well, yes, I do. It wouldn't be the first time I'd opened on just a few hours of sleep, but I tried not to make a habit of it.

I edged next to Aaron at the bar while I waited on Andy to finish running his last load of dishware. I whispered and nodded in the direction of Larissa and her friends. "You see them? Larissa was talking to a high school kid before they got here. I don't know what was going on, but I got the feeling that it was not something good."

Aaron brushed off my concern. "The high school kids are always trying to get college students to buy beer and slip it to them around the corner. They never get away with it, but it doesn't stop them from asking."

"I don't know…" I watched as Larissa and her friends laughed at their table. "It seemed like more. Maybe I should tell Andy?"

"Really? It's not like he has a murder to investigate."

"I just..." I just hate it when he's right. "What if it is something important?"

"What if it turns out some goofball senior was just taking his shot and asking her to prom? Do you want to be known as the person who turned in two people for having a conversation?" He cut me off before I could answer. "There is no way that it wouldn't get out with your name attached to it. There is no such that as confidential in Baseless."

Andy emerged from the kitchen looking worse for the wear after a shift of bussing tables and washing dishes. "Let's go, Poppy, and the next time I suggest drinks at the taproom, tell me no."

Aaron reached out for a fist bump with Andy. "I really would have been sunk tonight if it wasn't for you. Calum is out of town, Deidre called in sick, and I don't like Cam working more than a couple of hours after school. Any normal Thursday would've been no problem—there must have been a full moon or something. It was wild."

I thought back to the conversation held in the shadows and the group of teens walking away from the taproom. "Yep, it was definitely a wild and weird night."

BLURRY EYED, I started coffee as soon as I entered the truck. Jake came in a few minutes behind me. "Whoa! Did you go out last night?"

"What?" I couldn't even gather the energy to let him know how rude his comment was.

"I mean, you just..." He gestured widely in my direction. "Kind of look..."

"Taproom." I muttered.

"Ohhhh," he said, "that explains it. You've got to pace yourself."

I slugged back some coffee, burning my tongue and throat. "I wasn't drinking. I was working."

Jake tilted his head like a confused puppy. "I thought the food truck was doing really well."

I pulled ingredients from the cooler and began setting my daily *mise en place* for the breakfast run. "It's doing great. And so, apparently, is the taproom. They were short-handed last night and got slammed, so I stepped in to help."

He nodded his head and started heating up the grill. "It was really busy when I drove by last night. I saw Larissa's car and thought it was probably something her sorority was doing."

"No, just really busy. She was talking to some kids outside."

"Ris?" He laughed. "Talking to kids? Doubtful. She thinks that kids are 'money-sucking, life-ending, disease vectors.'"

"Yikes, that's quite an opinion. But it wasn't *kid* kids, not little ones, but teens. From the high school. I thought it was weird."

"Maybe a little bit... was she talking to them, or were they talking to her?"

"What do you mean? They were talking to each other."

"Okay, what would be weird," Jake countered. "Is if Ris walked up and started a conversation with somebody from the high school. Her thoughts on little kids are positively gentle compared to her thoughts on small town high schools. But it is not unheard of for high schoolers to come up and start talking to her."

"Really? What about her says 'talk to me?'"

"Girls who are hoping to get in her sorority, usually legacies, see her necklace and start talking all the time. It is rarer with guys, but sometimes they will ask her out."

I thought about what I'd witnessed the night before. "That's what Aaron said—"

"You told Aaron?" His voice turned sharp.

"Well, yes, it happened outside his business and it seemed weird—"

"Lots of things seem weird, it doesn't necessarily make them wrong."

"Aaron said the guy was probably trying to get her to buy him beer."

"That happens, too."

"He said I shouldn't bother Andy."

Jake popped open the window and took the first order for the day. "That's your cop friend, right? You definitely shouldn't bother him. You don't want to get a reputation as a narc."

I took another slug of coffee and tried to shake the cobwebs out of my head. "Aaron said that, too."

Jake reached around me to grab drinks from the cooler. "Then I'd say your friend is a lot smarter than he looks."

I nodded my head in agreement. "You guys are probably right. I mean…. sometimes I talk to kids from the high school and I'm never up to no good. We're not that much older than them and… I need to forget about it."

Jake clipped two more orders to the board. "What you need to do is get cooking."

12

M y mind wandered as I put in my final supply order for Bluebonnet Trails weekend. Local campgrounds were filling up, and a city crew was busy marking off vendor spaces in the town square. Our idyllic little town was about to explode into a small city for 48 hours. Even people who didn't take part in the bike race would pour into town for the festival—because Baseless knows how to put on a party.

I looked up the expected number of visitors, then the weather forecast for the weekend. I checked the calendar to count how many weekends we were out from Easter. Then I re-calculated the visitor numbers and estimated how many of those would stop at my food truck.

That's a big number.

Now, the majority are going to want the Lone Star burger —my special for the weekend. Many of those will want fries. I thought about how many individual pieces of crispy potato would pass through my serving window and then shut it out of my mind. Some things are too big to consider. Now, what about the vegans... I calculated the time it takes to make a vegan patty from scratch and ordered the pre-made patties from my supplier. They won't taste as good, but there's only so much I can do. Jake has been a big help, but I really need someone with lots of kitchen experience for a weekend like this. It is more than just passing breakfast tacos through the window to my regulars. I need everything to run smoothly; I need every food item that goes out to be perfect, because I never know who will be on the receiving end.

I sent an email to Queen of Tarts with my bread order—the best soft, seeded hamburger buns in the state, plus some gluten-free, dairy-free buns that are better than edible. I added some individually wrapped bluebonnet cookies for good measure. They are delicious and I would be happy to eat any leftover stock. I placed a sticky note on my calendar to remind myself to pull myself a cookie, because deep down, I knew there was no chance of leftovers.

The more I dug into my planning—double checking numbers, order dates, and schedules—the more my mind drifted away from Bluebonnet Trails weekend and back to Sarah. As much as I missed having Kim by my side, Sarah would have been able to get the job done. She had a rare talent, and they had extinguished it because she was at my food truck.

I think.

Andy had called earlier to let me know that Sarah's family had been cleared of suspicion. Their church had been holding an all-night prayer service, and it was livestreamed. Video clearly showed the Pastor and Mother, as well as the two younger children, in the church for hours before and after someone had killed Sarah. Several people confirmed their presence, and the tech crew had been through everything, sure that the video and time stamps were legitimate. There is no way they could have been involved in her death.

That brought them back to the idea that it was an attempted robbery gone wrong. With no leads, no suspects, it was the best they had. Short of a miracle—or Baseless PD deciding to arrest me—there would be no arrest. No conviction. No justice. I mirthlessly wondered if in a few years the local ghost tours would swing by and tell the tragic tale of a girl whose soul wanders aimlessly in search of her killer.

Without consciously making the decision to go out there, I found myself pulling into the parking lot at First Family Free Fellowship. I sat for a moment, thinking about what I expected to gain from making the drive. I had no hope to offer them, and they had nothing but disdain for me.

I watched a woman working the flowerbeds near the back door. Even with my limited view, I knew she was smiling. I could read it in her body language as she lovingly placed each plant, patting the soil around their bases. Pallets of different flowers and greenery sat along the sidewalk, promising that the completed project would be more than a few petunias and colored mulch. The woman stretched her arms and lifted herself to standing, unstable from the time spent on her knees as she worked the soil. She turned and walked to my car.

Mother.

She tapped on the window. "Do come and visit while I work."

I rolled the window down, unsure of how to explain my presence. "I'm sorry, I shouldn't be here. I don't know why—"

"Pshaw—," she waved her dirt encrusted, gloved hands in a circle. "I knew you'd come; I just didn't know when. Now, please, come and see Cassandra's garden."

Intrigued, I left the car to follow her. "I heard," I stumbled with the words. "About the video, I mean, and…"

"Yes," She motioned to a stack of bagged gravel for me to sit on as she dropped back to the ground. "They've had it for some time, but I suppose they have to check everything out. Some people might be angry, but not me. It assures me they are taking Casey's death seriously and gives me hope they will find the person responsible."

I was not expecting to hear that. "I'm angry."

"Yes," she nodded. "I can see it in you. But you aren't angry at the police, or at us, you are angry with yourself. And that, my child, is misplaced."

I wiped away at the tears that threatened to leak from my eyes. "I'm angry at whoever killed Sarah, but I'm also angry I put her in that place."

Mother held a plant to her nose and sniffed deeply, then she held it out to me. "Do you recognize this?"

I squinted at the plant, then reached over to pinch off a tiny leaf. "It's lemon thyme."

She nodded enthusiastically. "Yes, this was always one of Casey's favorites. Anything that had the slightest bit of citrus to it, she loved. This is her garden."

"A memorial garden?"

"No, I don't like the word 'memorial,' I call it a memory garden. A memorial reminds you of something that *was*, a memory *is*. She was away from us for so long, but not gone. She is away from us again, but not gone. We'll see her again." She glanced at the notes neatly written in a spiral notebook at her side, then reached for another plant. "When Casey was with us, working in the garden was one of her favorite things. She wanted to know about all the plants—how people used them in the past, how they related to other plants, how we could make them grow bigger and healthier."

"That's why she was so good at flavor pairings!"

Mother grinned. "Yes, she didn't just have book knowledge, she understood the plants on another level. In a different time in history, she probably would have been a healer, a medicine woman. With a drugstore on every corner, that practice is almost gone. She turned her knowledge—her love—to using her plants for cooking."

"What will you do with the garden?"

"It is a living memory for me. It will change a bit each season, of course, but everything in it will remind me of my daughter who is away." She plucked a basil leaf and popped it in her mouth. "I will make the herbs available to families who use our food pantry. Anything that isn't used fresh will be dried and stored for the future. And, of course, you will always be welcome to the herbs grown here."

"Why would you do that? Why are you being so nice to me?"

She shrugged. "I have no reason not to be anything but kind. You showed great kindness to my daughter, and it is obvious that you though fondly of her. If things had turned out differently…"

"Aren't you angry at her? She ruined your lives when she went into foster care and has almost tanked your business all these years later."

"She saved our lives," sadness wrinkled her face. "We were not bad parents; we just weren't good parents. We were so young when she was born, and then there was such a large age gap between her and the next two… it was just *hard*. She acted out because she needed more attention than we were giving her. Unfortunately, while in foster care she just learned more about manipulation and she lost her way. At the same time, we found our way. We really started to study the Word. We took the state-mandated parenting classes, then I enrolled in child development classes and psychology classes. We didn't just study, we applied all that knowledge to becoming good parents to all three of our kids."

My chest was tight as I listened to the pain in her voice. "Then why didn't they let her come back? Why did she not want anything to do with you after she aged out of foster care?"

"We were too late." She continued lovingly placing the plants. "The pre-teen and teen years are difficult with any child. Life in our home was evolving, and she didn't always like it. Some of the foster homes were good for her and some were not, but the bouncing back and forth? That was always bad. Then... there was Larissa. At a point we had to make a choice—we could let Cassandra go for the sake of the two youngest, or we could risk losing all three of them."

"You just let her go?"

"There's not a day that has gone by that I don't wonder if we made the right choice." She wiped at the tears on her cheeks, leaving muddy trails. "I live my life evaluating everything I did from the moment I found out I was carrying her, looking for the one thing I should have done differently to change the outcome. Did I eat fish when I was pregnant? Was it the disposable diapers? Should I have pushed her harder when she wanted to give up gymnastics at age ten? What if we had moved far away from Lubbock—someplace for a new start, someplace where there was no Larissa?"

We sat in silence, both lost in our thoughts. I finally cleared my throat and asked the question that had been weighing on me. "Do you think Larissa could be involved?"

She closed her eyes, and her cheek spasmed as she held back emotion. "Those girls loved each other. They were a bad match—nothing but trouble—but absolutely friends to the end. I do not believe that there is any situation in which Larissa would knowingly do harm to Casey." She opened her eyes and stared into mine. "But she absolutely might be involved with someone who would do harm to Casey."

I stood from the bags of gravel and dusted myself off. "I am so, so sorry... for everything. I wish—"

"Don't wish. We can't change the past, but we can do something about the future. Live your life in a way that you can be proud of and remember Casey—Sarah—as the vibrant and talented young lady she was becoming. The guilty party may never be found, but we can find justice by celebrating the little bit of good life she had."

13

One thing you don't think about with a food truck is washing it. Of course, you must keep the inside impeccably clean—it is a kitchen, after all. Most food truck owners know that the counter where orders are passed over is an extension of that and requires special care. During a festival weekend, several thousand people will touch the counter without a thought about all those that came before. I've witnessed enough people not wash their hands upon leaving a public restroom to know what that means.

But the outside of the truck? I soon realized that without regular washing, it starts to look run down and aged. You can't just drive it through the automatic carwash, so I had invested in a portable system and a ladder that would allow me to get to the top of the truck. I had special polish to keep it shiny, and a conditioner to apply to my window awning to keep the colors bright and vibrant. I had everything I needed to keep it in tip-top shape.

Except the zeal to do it.

Washing the truck was the least favorite of all my duties, which is why Kim usually took the lead and I turned assistant for the day. I almost didn't answer the call when her name popped up on the screen. I knew what she was going to say.

"Is the truck ready?"

I pretended to not know what she meant. "Well, our orders won't be delivered until closer to the weekend. You know how I am about fresh ingredients. I will get the meat a day earlier because I need to—"

"Poppy," she used the same tone she did when her kids had gone too far. "You know I'm not asking about deliveries."

"I've got a back-up hotspot for the credit card machine, and extra change from the bank."

"Also, not what I'm asking." She waited for me, but I wasn't about to volunteer anything. "You need to wash the truck. Today."

I thought about the steps involved and immediately needed a nap. "I think it will be fine, just this once—"

"Sure, it will probably be better if it looks like all those trucks that travel with the carnival rides. Maybe you could unscrew some of the bulbs in the sign? Just to make it look authentic."

JAKE HADN'T BEEN GONE from the truck very long when I'd called to see if he could come back to help wash. He had been happy for the extra hours when I spoke to him, but now that he was here, he seemed less than eager.

"Look," I said, "it's okay if you have something else going on. You don't have to stay."

There was a flash of something—anger? frustration?—across his facial features. "No, I'm fine. I said I'd work, and I'm working. What do we need to do?"

"If you can go up the ladder and use the brush on the top, then I can do the lower part of the truck." I tried to sound enthusiastic. "Unless you want a laugh, in which case you can let the short girl try to scrub the top."

"I'll do the top," there was the tiniest of smiles. "Although I seem to remember something about a previous assistant falling off a ladder in your presence, so maybe you should stand over by the tree."

"Hey! I had nothing to do with that." I handed the scrub brush to him as he climbed the ladder. "And she wasn't on a ladder which was the entire problem. She'd stacked boxes up to climb on instead of waiting for help."

"Classic short girl," he called down. "Sarah used to do stuff like that all the time. She never wanted to ask anyone for help."

I took the brush as he climbed down and moved the ladder to access the next patch of roof. "It seems like independence was important to her."

"Probably from being in foster care. She didn't know how to let people in."

I pondered his words while he scrubbed. "But she and Larissa? They were very close. Her mom said they loved each other."

Jake stopped scrubbing and looked down at me. "What? When did her mother say that?"

"Yesterday…" There was no reason to feel guilt, but it washed over me anyway. "I kind of found myself at their church and she was there—"

"What else did she say?" He climbed down the ladder, no longer even pretending to clean. "Did she talk about anyone else?"

"No," I stepped to switch off the motor on the washer. "She just told me about when Sarah was Cassandra—when she was young. She told me how the girls became friends, and the trouble they got into, but I asked if she thought Larissa could be involved—"

"What?" he seemed incredulous. "You don't really believe that she would murder Sarah?"

I wasn't sure what I believed, but I knew that Larissa was the only person who kept popping up over and over. The only person with questionable habits and a drawer of cash. I wanted to tell Jake what I'd seen and heard in the apartment, but I didn't want to endure another lecture, which seemed to be a habit of all males over the age of 12 when dealing with a petite, young woman. "No, I don't think so, but—hey! I just thought of something! You remember that zip code I found in Sarah's glove box? Don't y'all's apartments use keypads for entry?"

Jake squinted in confusion as he tried to follow my train of thought. "Yes, but that wasn't Sarah's code."

"Could it be someone else's code?"

He shook his head. "Nah, maybe her lockout code?"

"To lock the door?"

"No, those doors seem neat, but they don't really work that well. Each apartment has a master code that they use for maintenance, and you can use yours if you get locked out of your apartment. It can't be turned off."

"That sounds dangerous."

"Not really. The office gets an alert if the lockout code is used."

My stomach sank. "Really? They know whenever someone goes in an apartment?"

Jake laughed. "I don't think they really pay that much attention. It doesn't matter anyway, it's not her code."

I was walking a dangerous line. "You're probably right. I should just forget about it."

"That's probably best." The motor hummed to life at the flip of the switch, and Jake ascended the ladder to renew his efforts at scrubbing the truck roof.

∽

WE SAT at one of the outdoor tables, admiring our handiwork as the sun glinted off the food truck. I would never admit it to Kim, but food out of a shiny truck really does taste better.

Aaron strode over with two flights of the April brews and a basket of chips. "Enjoy." He didn't sound like he meant it, and when the second flight tipped off the tray and onto Jake... well, I am pretty sure Aaron meant that.

"Oh—" Jake let forth a string of curses as he jumped from the table and ripped off his beer-soaked shirt. I stared, wordlessly, as he wrung the liquid onto the ground. I wouldn't say he was *covered* in tattoos, but he had several, and most did not seem to be part of the Tweety Bird and Taz variety. He quickly pulled his shirt back on when he caught me staring. "I told you I have some past reminders I don't like to share with the world."

Embarrassed that he had caught me, I try to justify my staring. "I thought you probably had track mark scaring, or something like that—"

He laughed. "No way! Needles were not my game. Well, not that kind of needle. Obviously, tattoo needles were." He stared off into the distance. "It's not the idea of tattoos that bothers me. It's the fact that I didn't always make the best choices when considering what I would permanently ink on my body." He pulled his shirt up to expose his left ribs, boldly sporting SS Bolts. "Like this. It was a dare, and the payoff was dope. Let's just say, it doesn't represent who I am."

Aaron returned with a bar towel and another flight. "Sorry about that, man." I scowled at him and he retreated into the taproom.

I turned back to Jake. "Can't you get them removed?"

He let out a long sigh. "Well... the only habit more expensive than getting tattoos is getting them removed. I'm planning on getting laser treatment on some of them, and others I'm going to get covered up with new—less stupid—artwork."

"Sounds like it's a long process."

"It is a long process." he raised one glass to me. "But I'm on a new path and I have a closet full of long-sleeved shirts to see me through it. Cheers."

I tipped my glass to his and then chewed on a chip while I let my mind wander. Eventually, as it always seemed to do, it came back to Sarah. "What do you know about Abigail?"

"I don't know her, but I know people just like her. Trap house hos are all the same."

My jaw dropped at his assessment. "Don't you think that is kind of harsh? Especially for someone you don't know!"

"You don't get it," he motioned to our peaceful setting. "I bet you've never lived outside of this kind of life." I wanted to tell him he was wrong, but he wasn't. "You might know some casual drug users—they snorted half a line of coke at a club in Dallas, or they passed a joint at summer camp. Abigail's house was the kind of place I used to hang out at. It was all about drugs—usually meth or crack—buying, selling, and using. She was a pass-through, it came to her already packaged, and she sent it out to the streets. Anyone who sold or delivered was paid in product. They paid her in product. If they couldn't keep the lights on, somebody would turn tricks to pay the bill. It's not like it is on TV—there are no bricks of cash in the walls, and no high-dollar homes. It is dirty, gritty, and depressing."

I cleared my throat. "Why would Sarah stay there?"

"She thought she could hide," his lips quirked into a smile.

"Do you think the murder could involve Abigail?"

This got a full-throated laugh. "No way! I'd be surprised if she's left the house more than twice in the last year. That's another thing that is not like the movies—junkies don't have the ambition to commit a pre-meditated crime. And she wouldn't come up just to say hello." He tapped his hands nervously on the table. "Face it, Poppy, they will never find out who killed Sarah. You might as well give up, too, because nothing good can come out of digging around."

14

"Are you comfortable? Do you need another pillow?"

Kim waved her arms around her head like she was warding off a swarm of particularly hungry mosquitoes. "I'm fine! Quit fussing and let's get to work."

I moved to the other side of the kitchen and began pulling ingredients from the refrigerator. "I just don't want to send you home in worse condition that I picked you up."

Kim smiled broadly. "Just don't push me down the stairs again."

"I did not push you down the stairs!" I gasped. "There aren't even stairs anywhere near the walk-in, you—"

"You know this town loves a good story and what sounds better—I fell off a stack of boxes or you pushed me down the stairs? Just imagine what my tip jar is going to look like when I get back to work."

I scowled at her. "You may not have a job if you keep saying I pushed you down the stairs."

Kim let out a laugh. "Oh? I didn't realize Jake was doing such a good job that my return would be in jeopardy."

"He's not." I sighed. "Well, all things considered, he's doing fine."

"'All things considered' meaning for someone who knows nothing about food or cooking?"

I nodded. "Exactly. Don't get me wrong—I appreciate the help, but it's not the same as having you there."

"Or Sarah." We sat quietly with our sense of loss for something we never really had. "Andy told me that the parents have been definitively cleared."

I recounted my trip to Waco and discussion with Sarah's mother. "She seemed... at peace, I guess. The whole situation is so weird, and I don't quite know what to make of them, but I guess that doesn't matter. It's not against the law to be strange."

"Strange people sometimes do things that are against the law," Kim countered.

"Perhaps, but video proof says that they didn't kill Sarah."

Kim chewed on her lower lip. "Could they have sent someone else to do it? Their whole set-up seems kind of cult-y—"

"I think they truly believed they could get through to her. Why send someone to murder her if they could just buy her off?" I stood in front of the large whiteboard in my kitchen, trying to remember what recipe we were supposed to work on today. I wrote "SARAH" in the center.

"No," Kim said. "Put the names in order—Cassandra, Molly, Sarah—and connect them with arrows."

The recipe forgotten, we soon had the board filled with names and connections to each of the names that Sarah had gone by. I pointed to Larissa's name. "She's the only one who knew all three names."

"That's not right," Kim said. "Jake said he knew her real name and knew she had gone by Molly."

"He knew she'd used those names, but he didn't know her when she was going by those names. It was after-the-fact knowledge."

"But he's known Larissa for a long time?"

"I don't think…" I stopped to sift through all the snippets of conversations I'd had with Jake. "I don't really know how long he's known her. I've never asked that, just how well he knows her." Kim raised her eyebrows at me, encouraging me to continue. "'Moderately well' is what he said. He calls her Ris, which seems to imply some familiarity."

"If he knew Larissa before, wouldn't he have known Sarah?"

"If Sarah's parents are to be believed, yes. But I'm not sure how much of their talk about Larissa is just a way to shift blame. They didn't seem that close to me—Sarah was usually with Jake; I hardly saw Larissa until after the murder."

Kim grabbed her crutches and made her way over to the whiteboard. She drew a line through Sarah's parents. "They eliminated them as suspects. They were probable, but not possible." She drew a box around the name of William Wrinkle. "He hasn't been cleared, so is still possible, but not probable."

"We can eliminate Jake. He's been cleared, he got there right before me."

Her hand hovered over his name. "Where was he before that?"

"He dropped Sarah off, started to drive home, then realized she left her phone in the car. He made a loop around at Pecan."

"Is he on any surveillance tape in the area?" She drew a box around his name. "Unless that can be proven, he is possible, not probable."

I picked up another marker. "In that case…" I drew my name and put a box around it. "I'm also possible, not probable. I came up on the scene at about the same time as William and Jake."

Kim narrowed her eyes at me. "True. It's hard to believe you'd murder anyone, but I also never would have thought you to be the kind of person to push me down the stairs."

"I didn't—" Kim's laughter halted my protest. I was glad she was feeling better, but things were still a bit too raw for me. I turned back to the whiteboard. "That leaves us with Abigail and Larissa, and a possible unknown assailant."

Kim drew large circles around their names, then hobbled back to the table. She hoisted her leg into a second chair and took a long drink of iced tea, the small bit of exertion having taken a toll on her. "So, of those three—our possible and probable group—what do we know? Only one person knew all three incarnations of Sarah. Abigail knew two—"

"No, she only knew her as Molly." I closed my eyes and replayed my visit to the trap house. "Not really even as Molly, she called her Cookie... and I shocked her when I told her what had happened."

"She appeared shocked," Kim clarified. "It's not like she would have said, 'Oh, right, I knew that because I killed her.'"

"Our third possible and probable didn't know her at all." I said. "Unless they did. Which we have no way of knowing because we have no idea who it might be."

The noise of a car door closing brought us back to reality. I grabbed a dishrag and ran to the board, erasing the names and quickly writing down some random ingredients. The front door creaked open, and a familiar voice called out, "Helloooo. Are you ready, sis?"

Kim and I looked quickly around the kitchen, making sure there was no evidence of our sleuthing. I called out, "Hey, Andy, come on back, we're just finishing up." I threw ingredients back into the fridge and clean dishes into the sink.

He entered the kitchen with a puzzled look on his face. "It's so clean in here."

"Andrew!" Kim scolded. "Poppy always keeps a clean kitchen!"

He had the good grace to look embarrassed. "I didn't mean it that way. Usually when you guys have been working on a recipe, there's evidence. Smells, samples, work out on the counter…"

"Evidence?" I croaked. "You hear that, Kim? Now he's treating us like one of his cases."

She humphed in reply. "If you must know, Mr. can't-let-the-day-job-go, we spent most of the time brainstorming, and the few things we tried didn't quite pan out. So, no 'evidence' as you put it."

"To tell you the truth," Kim narrowed her eyes at my words. "We spent a lot of the time just catching up. We used to see each other every day, so we had a lot of words backed up and waiting to come out."

"Yes," Kim smiled. "We had a lot of catching up to do. Now you need to take me home because Poppy has a date."

"A date?" Andy looked at me like I'd grown a third arm.

"No, not a date," I swatted at Kim with my dishcloth. "Aaron and I are going bowling in Fulfur. We're just blowing off a little steam before things go crazy this weekend."

Andy nodded slowly. "Sure, I get that. You can't date someone you've known since elementary school, right?"

"Exactly!" I was emphatic. "Kim thinks every time I'm within three feet of a male, it is a date. Going on a date with Aaron would be so wrong—like going on a date with you!"

"Oh, absolutely," he laughed. "That's just… crazy talk."

Kim watched us for a moment and then used her crutches to heft herself up. "Alright, I'm ready for my police escort home." She smiled at me. "Since the incident, I've had to have a police escort when leaving the house."

Andy looked confused. "What incident?"

I walked to the front door and opened it. "Andy, take your sister home."

∾

AARON DRIED his hands and picked up his bowling ball, lining up on the lane. "So, what did you and Kim create today?"

"A murder board."

He looked back at me, eyes wide, just as he released his ball. It spun into the gutter and dropped into the return. "I'm sorry—what? I thought you guys were working on a special recipe for next month's Highland Games."

I carefully lined up and released the ball, spinning it smoothly down the boards. "We were, but somewhere between getting the ingredients out and Andy picking her up, we started trying to figure out who killed Sarah."

"And what did you decide?"

I grabbed my ball from the return and lined up again. "We're pretty sure we know who *didn't* kill Sarah. But we still have three people we can't eliminate."

I could see that Aaron was struggling with what to say next. "I don't think it is safe for you to be investigating a murder. You could—"

I held up a palm to stop him. "I've already heard this from Andy, I don't need a repeat. We aren't investigating, we were just discussing. If you want to talk about my safety, how about the fact that I won't feel safe until we know who did it?"

"Pops," he put his hands on my shoulders. "I'm right next door. The whole crew is, and we're not going to let anything happen to you."

I looked up, finally letting my guard down. "You aren't there at five o'clock in the morning. It's just me and whoever is working." I felt my heart hammer in my chest. "What if we'd both been there that morning? Could I have stopped it, or would the body count have been two instead of one? Until we know who killed Sarah, and why they killed Sarah, I don't think anyone in this town is safe."

"Time for a break." He led me to the table and pressed the button to signal we were ready to order food. "Why didn't you say something earlier? I knew it upset you—everybody in town was upset—but I had no idea you were worried about your safety. The cops seemed to think it was just someone passing through town, easy access off the highway."

"Do they? It seems like an easy way to write-off a case they can't solve. 'Oops, the killer already left town, so everybody go back to normal life.'"

He placed our order with the waitress and then leaned across the table. "I don't think you are being fair to Andy."

"It's not just Andy!" The frustration was growing. "The DPS and PD are working the case, and no one seems to be interested in the two prime suspects!"

"Come again? I thought they had already eliminated all of their suspects. You know, through alibis and evidence and stuff."

"Larissa is up to something." I crossed my arms and sank back into the seat.

"You can't go around accusing people of stuff!" Aaron leaned across the table and dropped his voice to a whisper. "If word gets around that you are a narc, your business is sunk."

I glared at him. "A narc. A *narc*? Are you kidding me? We're talking about a murder, not buying beer for a 17-year-old."

Aaron dragged his hands through his hair. "That's exactly what I'm talking about! You saw her talking to a high school kid and now you're convinced she is a stone-cold killer."

"It's more than that, it's…." It suddenly occurred to me I'd said too much.

"It's what?"

"Nothing."

"Poppy." He stared me down.

"Fine. She has a drawer full of cash in her bedroom. Not like I'm-stashing-my-birthday-money cash, but bricks, thousands of dollars."

"And how—" Aaron paused to smile as the server

dropped our food on the table. "How, exactly, do you know what she has in her bedroom?"

I picked at my food before quietly answering. "I might have gone in the apartment while she wasn't there and—"

"You broke into her apartment?"

"No! I used the code from Sarah's glove box to get in—"

"Why were you in Sarah's car?"

I was regretting this conversation more with each word. "Let's focus on the important stuff. Larissa has been getting Sarah into trouble since junior high. Larissa is up to something sketchy around the taproom—which should concern you. Larissa has thousands of dollars stashed in her apartment. She is not innocent."

"It's a long way from 'not innocent' to killer." Aaron pressed the call button again and asked the server to close out our tab and our lane.

"Wow." I stood, then remembered my stupid bowling shoes. I sat back down to change. "The road from 'I'll never let you get hurt' to 'Don't be a narc' is awfully short."

"The reason I don't want you to go around accusing people is because I don't want you to get hurt!" The group in the next lane turned to look at us, and Aaron realized his voice was pitching louder. He dropped back down to a strained whisper. "You need to stay out of it. I'll ask around and see if anyone knows why some kids from the high school would talk to her. But you have to stop… whatever it is you think you're doing. Please."

I slapped some bills down by my plate and left.

15

There was a light tap on the door of the food truck. "We're closed!" I yelled, double checking that the sign was off, and the windows closed. The locked doorknob rattled, and my heart pounded.

"Hey, Poppy? It's just me—Cam." I opened the door to Aaron's youngest brother. "Aaron sent me up to see if you need help." He looked down at his feet and mumbled. "And tell you to quit pouting and just use the big kitchen already."

I thought about trying to mix several hundred pounds of seasoned burger meat in the commercial kitchen at the brewery versus the same task in my 16x7 box. "Thank you for the offer, but I'm fine. My workspace is perfectly adequate for my needs and I don't need any help."

Cam sank into himself in a way that only a 15-year-old can properly accomplish. "Can I stay here anyway? Aaron is in a really bad mood today."

A part of me was happy that Aaron was unhappy, but Cam didn't deserve to be caught up in adult drama. "Sure, come in and shut the door. Make sure you lock it."

He settled on a stool in the corner. "Is it scary to be here by yourself?"

I skinned and seeded my charred poblano peppers and began chopping. "No, I've been here by myself a lot. It's like being at home."

"But Sarah got killed here."

"Bad things happen. I can't shut down because of it." I was glad that I had an excuse not to meet his eyes as I worked.

"There's been a lot of bad things happening." The sadness in his voice was heartbreaking. "I don't even want to go to school anymore."

"What?" I turned to face him. "You love school! What about baseball? You guys are doing great this season."

He shook his head. "It was great. Now all people want to talk about is what happened to Rhys. And the whole school suspects all the baseball players, even though none of us had anything to do with it. Most of us on JV barely even knew him! I mean, it's sad and all, but... I just want things to go back to how they were."

I moved the bowl of peppers aside and began chopping pecans. "I get it. Everybody wants to talk about what happened to Sarah, too. I just want to know why it happened —who did it. I bet you feel the same way about Rhys."

He nodded. "Then people will stop talking about me and the rest of the team."

"I hope we both get our names cleared soon."

THE AFTERNOON WENT by more quickly with Cam in the truck. When I started weighing meat and forming patties, he jumped up to work. He didn't need instructions and didn't need to talk. His quiet company was exactly what I needed. We carried the sealed containers of patties down to the refrigerated walk-in together.

"I'm supposed to work the whole weekend, so I can help if you need me to bring stuff to the truck," he said.

"That's what I'm for," we both jumped as Jake and Larissa rounded the corner of the brewery.

Cam stiffened. "I was just offering—"

"I may," I interjected. "Need you to help bring up supplies if we get really busy. And I definitely need you checking on the tables during the day."

Cam offered a small smile. "I know. You like to make sure I wipe them down, so no one is sitting at a sticky table. I'll set a timer, so I don't forget, then I'll check if you need anything before I head back here."

Jake snorted. "I can't imagine it gets so busy you need a little kid—"

"Then your imagination is lacking," Aaron stepped out the back door of the brewery. "Bluebonnet Trails is 48 hours of chaos, and it takes everyone working together to pull it off. If you aren't capable of that, take off now instead of leaving Poppy in a crunch when the time gets here."

Cam edged closer to his brother, and Jake puffed up his chest and widened his stance. I could practically hear David Attenborough doing a voiceover— "Here we see the male of the species partaking in a ridiculous show of aggression as they each feel threatened by scheduling issues, while ignoring the fact that the town is currently overrun with a criminal element distributing drugs and murdering people."

Wait. I glanced at Larissa, who stood glaring, arms crossed, as she waited on Jake. Could the drugs at the high school and Sarah's murder be connected? If Larissa was selling drugs that would explain the money. If Sarah found out, that could explain the murder.

"Well?!" Jake's voice dragged me back to the present. "I said I was just coming to get my check. Is it ready?"

"Oh, sure, it's up in the truck." I locked the door on the

walk-in and started to leave. I was stopped by the sound of Aaron's voice.

"What are you guys doing back here anyway?"

Larissa finally spoke up. "We saw a guy head this way, and he looked sketch."

"It was Sarah's stalker." Jake piped in.

"Right, Jake thought it was that stalker guy, so we followed him, but he was gone by the time we got around to the other side."

Aaron stared for a moment, clearly wanting to tell them to stay away, but aware he'd look like a huge jerk since they said they were following a suspicious person. "Will is a customer here, so don't bother him. If you think you see something suspicious, report it."

Cam piped up, his voice cracking. "If you see something, say something!"

Larissa snorted. "I'll meet you back at the car, Jake."

Jake nodded and headed to pick up his check. I couldn't think of a way to be cool about it, so I finally blurted out, "Why are you with Larissa?"

He stopped and looked around furtively. "I'll tell you when we're in the truck."

True to his word, he made one last look out the window after I handed him his check and said, "I thought about what you said about Larissa and Abigail working together. I don't think Larissa would hurt Sarah, but maybe they knew some-one…. I don't know, I just thought that if I could talk to her more, I could find out."

"And did you," I stuttered. "Find out, I mean."

"No," he shook his head. "Not really. I tried to get her talking about Sarah, but she got really upset and started crying."

"Could that be from guilt?"

"Maybe? I think she just misses her, like I do. Everybody is telling me that I need to move on and try to forget what happened, but how can you forget something like that? Every day of my life I will remember that morning."

"I know. I can't forget it either, I don't think I can move on until they find out who killed Sarah. Between that and the OD at the high school, Baseless just doesn't feel the same. I want to fix it."

"You can't fix it," Jake said. "Nobody can fix it, it's done."

"I know it can't be undone, but we need answers! I won't stop asking questions until my name is cleared."

"Okay," he said, "Consider us partners in crime, or partners in defeating crime, whatever."

"Really?" I asked. "You are not going to tell me to stop playing detective and leave it alone?"

He laughed. "Hasn't that already been tried? You obviously aren't going to listen, so I might as well join you—it is for Sarah, after all." He fell quiet for a moment. "I loved her more than anything, more than anyone. I hope she knew that I'd do anything for her."

I didn't know the answer, but I knew what Jake needed to hear. "I'm sure she did.

~

I CALLED Kim on my way home. "Can you try to find out more about Abigail?"

"Well, I'm gonna need more than that to go on."

"I don't have much, her first name and the address of the house. I could describe her.... maybe."

"What do you want to know?" Kim sounded more suspicious than curious.

"Her full name would be a start. If she's ever been arrested. Police calls to the house. If there is any connection to Larissa—"

"I know I shouldn't ask, but... why? What are you hoping to accomplish?"

I sighed. "I'm not sure. I feel like I'm so close to uncovering something important, but I don't know what it is. I need to find something to implicate her, or Larissa, or I need something to convince me they are not involved."

"Andy says Larissa hadn't left her apartment that morning."

"Really? When did he tell you that?"

She was quiet for a minute. "He didn't, exactly, tell me, but I overheard him talking to Walt. The electronic lock records show that the door was only opened once, and that would have been Sarah leaving the apartment."

"Is there any other proof?" I wanted badly to discount this new information.

"It's hard to prove a negative," Kim said. "She said she didn't leave her apartment and the electronic records show the door was only opened one time between midnight and 10 a.m."

"I know we're close." I was practically begging. "Just see if you can find out anything about Abigail, please."

16

I flipped through the mail, looking for anything that looked like a late notice. I work hard to keep things in line, but sometimes bills slip through the cracks. I need someone to help with the backend office work of running the truck. Or someone to help in the truck and free me up to take care of office work. I just need help.

A small, peach colored envelope caught my attention. It bore no return address, only my name and address neatly printed. The postmark showed it to have been mailed yesterday in Baseless.

I slowly inhaled through my nose and exhaled from my mouth as I fought to calm the jitters that overtook me at the sight of the envelope. I carefully slit open the top and slid out a notecard decorated with a watercolor floral design. Unremarkable, it was the same type of card you could buy boxes of at any store selling stationery products. Despite its mundane appearance, I still felt dread at opening the card.

The message was printed in the same neat handwriting as the address: You are in danger. There are bad people around you.

~

RATHER THAN SLEEPING, I tossed and turned as I thought about the mysterious correspondence. It was a warning, but it didn't sound like a threat. My first reaction had been to pick up the phone and call... who, exactly, would I call? The local police seemed to think I was the bad person. Andy and Trooper Moore had already warned me that investigating could put me in danger. My list of friends I could count on was already dangerously slim, and with Kim's broken leg and Aaron's broken attitude, it was downright bleak. So, I called no one, but tried to work out who would send me such a note.

Maybe it was a prank? None of my friends would inform me I was in danger through an anonymous note. Anyone who would contact me through an anonymous note wouldn't bother to warn me. I settled into my pillows and decided it must be a prank.

My relaxed state didn't last long as my phone sounded on my nightstand. I looked through blurry eyes—Aaron. There was no valid reason for Aaron to call at twelve after two in the morning, and I wasn't in the mood for a drunk dial. I declined the call. My phone immediately rang again. I answered and shouted at Aaron, "I still don't want to talk to you!"

The sound on the other end was chaos. I could hear shouts and sirens behind Aaron's terrified voice. "It's bad, Poppy, it's really bad—"

~

I COULD SEE the orange glow as soon as I turned east. By the time I reached Ron Road, flames were being replaced by thick smoke. I parked at The Tipsy Lady and ran down the street to the small crowd gathered behind the barrier that had been erected near St. Andrew's Brewery.

I pushed my way to Aaron, who was standing with several members of his family. "What happened?"

Mr. Martin faced me, his face stern, but eyes wet. "Looks like arson. Buildings don't look to be involved, but there could be damage."

"Why?" I choked on the smoke. "Why would anyone do this?"

A heavily dressed firefighter made his way to us and addressed the crowd. "I need the owner of—" Mr. Martin stepped forward. "—the food truck." All eyes turned to me. I stepped forward and timidly raised my hand. The firefighter looked at my bare feet and sneered. "Follow me—*carefully*." I followed him around the edge of the parking lot, the still smoldering grass attacking my lungs and eyes. "Stay here." He walked over to a fire truck and turned on the headlights, highlighting my food truck in its powerful beam.

Killer.

He cut the lights and stalked back to my side. "Do you know anyone who would do this?"

I couldn't see anything in the dark, but I still stared into the distance, picturing the word painted across the front of my business. I choked out an answer. "No."

"Well, the chance of the person who decorated your truck and the person who set the fire being two people is somewhere south of zero. We find your artist and we find the arsonist."

I slipped home and put on actual clothes—and shoes—before the fire department concluded their investigation and released the scene. Their judgment was simple—someone had doused the park in an accelerant to create a quick spreading, fast burning fire. Although it was technically just a green space belonging to the Martins, it was treated by the locals as a park. On sunny days it was filled with families playing games, picnicking, and just enjoying small town life. Now the green grass had streaks of black where the flames had ripped through, and any remaining flowers drooped as if they too were crying from loss.

My food truck stood in the middle of it and was obviously where the conflagration originated. Besides the accusatory artwork, black marks now snaked up the sides. The service window and door had warped from the intense heat, and the counter where I had passed thousands of meals had melted into a grotesque modern art sculpture. It was dubbed too dangerous for me to enter the interior and I was grateful for that.

The taproom and brewery were intact, but there was heavy smoke damage on the outside. The umbrellas covering the patio tables had tiny holes burned through them from the ash that floated like angry snow. Cosmetic damage, but damage, nonetheless.

Mr. Martin had rallied troops hours before daylight descended upon Baseless. I wasn't quite sure how he managed it, but by the time Jake showed up for work, the entire burned space was marked off with sawhorses and I was setting up in the brewery kitchen to handle our morning regulars.

"Whoa—" Jake gawked at the activity happening all around us. "What happened?"

Aaron stomped into the kitchen. "Poppy and her inability to stay out of things is what happened!"

I shouted back at him. "Excuse me?"

"You heard me!" A scowl covered the exhaustion on Aaron's face. "YOU are the reason for this. This was an attack on your business, and it just about took out ours, too. And guess what? Our whole family has put everything they have into this business and we don't have a trust fund to fall back on if it fails."

Jake stepped closer to me. "Hey, man, that's not fair. Poppy's whole life is centered around that food truck—"

"No, it's not, her whole *year* is centered on the truck. If it fails, she just goes back to the life she had before."

My body vibrated with anger. All this time I thought Aaron supported me and my vision, when in fact, he thought I was a kid at play. Rational thought went out the window and before I knew what was happening, the three of us were shouting at each other. No one could hear what anyone else was saying, and that was probably for the best, as I suspect that none of it was nice.

"Hey," Mr. Martin entered the kitchen from the back door. "HEY!" We stopped shouting and faced him. "This isn't helping anything. What's the problem?"

"He—" Jake pointed at Aaron.

Mr. Martin held up a hand. "Who are you?"

"Jake, I work in Poppy's truck."

"Great, Jake, go get set up in the front. You are going to take and serve orders at the bar today."

I gave a slight nod to Jake, and he reluctantly left to await the morning rush.

"Now," Mr. Martin surveyed us with knowing eyes. "Poppy, what did Aaron say to you?"

"Why do you think—" A stern look from Mr. Martin silenced Aaron's protestations.

"He implied that I am the one to blame for the fire."

Mr. Martin snorted. "The only person to blame for the fire is the idiot that soaked our grass in gasoline and put a match to it."

"It was a message to Poppy." Aaron insisted.

"So it was, but Poppy is not to blame. We cannot have fighting among the family and get through this." He stared at us until we both acknowledged his statement. "Aaron, take

Cam home to sleep a bit, then make sure he gets to school by third period." Aaron moved to protest but thought better of it. Mr. Martin faced me. "I'll get someone out to help you and the boy. The insurance adjuster is to be here by 9:00 and you'll need to be available."

Mr. Martin's speech had done nothing to quell the anger between me and Aaron. I turned back to setting my *mise en place* and for the first time wondered if the danger to me was closer to home than I'd ever imagined.

17

I scrubbed at the letters as tall as me, but the paint refused to be removed.

"Pops, what are you doing?" Aaron came around the side of the truck. "They are coming to tow this away in an hour."

"I know, but I need to get this off."

He stood; arms crossed. "It's going to the scrap yard. You're getting a new truck."

I continued to scrub. "I know."

He left, only to return a few minutes later, trailing a bright orange extension cord behind him. "Stand back."

I moved away, and he used the power washer to remove the offending word. Silently, he picked up the machine and headed back down the hill to the brewery.

It wasn't an apology, but it was a start.

I PASSED the envelope over to Kim.

"You do realize," she fussed. "That this could have been filled with anthrax or ricin or something else terrible."

"It wasn't."

"It could have been." She stared at the card. "You've got to show this to Andy."

"Why? So he can tell me to stay out of it?" I snatched the card back from her hands. "The warning came too late, but there is no threat here. I don't want advice; I just want someone to be upset with me."

"I am upset, you're being ridiculous."

"No, not upset *at* me, upset *with* me! This month has tested me in ways I never imagined and now—days before one of the biggest events of the year—I have no food truck."

"Aren't you going to use the taproom kitchen?"

"That's not the same." I shoved the envelope in my purse. "This was an opportunity to help cement my name, my truck, not the taphouse. I need someone who understands that, but it seems like I need to keep looking." I could hear Kim calling after me as I walked out the door, but I didn't slow down. I couldn't take another friend turning on me.

THIS TIME I wasn't timid when approaching the house. "Hey! Abigail! Open up!" I pounded on the door, the windows shaking each time my fist made contact with the cheap wood. After a few minutes, a man opened the door.

"What's the problem, man?"

"I need to speak to Abigail."

"Whatever." He opened the door wider and then disappeared back into the house.

I charged in behind him. "Abigail? Abigail! I need to talk to you about Sar—Molly!"

She staggered out of a room, her hand shaking as she tried to light a cigarette. She mumbled something and motioned for me to follow her. She plopped down at a kitchen table, knocking empty cans to the floor.

"What?"

"Who killed Sarah?"

She leaned back in the chair, pulling her fingers through her thin hair. "Who?"

"Molly! Cookie! Whatever you called her—"

Wincing at my loud voice, she shook her head in understanding. "Um, Cookie, I don't know. Some chick came by and told me she was dead—"

"I'm that chick!" Frustration bubbled out of me. "Somebody killed her. Somebody that knew her. Do you know who it might have been?"

Abigail took a long drag on her cigarette, her hands still shaking. "Yeah, probably. She was hiding from somebody." I nodded, encouraging her along. "She was scared when she came here, but she needed a place where nobody'd think to look."

"Why'd she leave?"

"That girl—the one that brought her here, she came for her."

"Do you know who the girl was? Was it Larissa?"

"I don't—" she looked around the room like she might find the answer in the stack of dirty dishes. "I don't remember her name, but Barry said she was cool."

I added another name to the ever-changing list of suspects. "Who's Barry?"

She smiled, her rotted teeth making me shudder. "Ya' know, Barry. He's the big man in charge."

"Your dealer?"

"Nah, we don't use words like that, that's low rent. He's the boss. I listen to what he says, and he makes sure I continue to live a life of luxury."

I looked around and wondered what she saw through her eyes. "Why would he have helped Cookie?"

"You're not listening. He wasn't helping *her*; the other chick was. Barry said this girl was coming by and she'd know the code. If she gave me the code, I was supposed to do whatever she said. She gave me the code and told me to take care of Cookie."

I thought about the new developments, trying to make sense of them. "What was the code?"

A gravelly laugh erupted from her. "I don't know! Doesn't matter. She knew it, so I took in Cookie. That little girl was scared, let me tell you. Jumped at her own shadow. After a bit she calmed down, would go out to the store and stuff. Then one day she just up and left with the other one."

"The one Barry said was okay?"

"Yep."

"What did Barry say about Cookie leaving?"

"Nothing. He didn't even know her. It was just a favor for the other girl."

I dug a scrap of paper from my purse and scribbled my number on it. "If you think of anything else, anyone who might have hurt Cookie, would you call me?"

She swayed in her chair. "Naw, I don't need to say anything that's going to bring cops around here."

"You can trust me." I reached across and clasped her arm. "I promise I won't lead the cops here. I'm just trying to find a killer."

I CALLED Kim on the way home. "Were you ever able to find out anything about Abigail, or the house in Austin?"

There was a pause while Kim considered her words. "Are we friends again? Because the last time we were talking, you walked out on me, and that's not what friends do."

"I'm sorry," I truly was. "I'm not doing the best job of handling stress right now. I shouldn't have walked out on you."

"I'm sorry, too," she responded. "I should've let you give the note to Andy."

"I'll call him when I get back to town."

"There's no need. I told him and he's probably waiting at your house." She took a deep breath. "So, what were you asking about the house in Austin?"

I decided that I'd be better off not responding to the revelation that she told Andy about the note. It was done and getting angry would just slow me down. "Were you able to find out who Abigail is, or anything about the house in Austin?"

"In short, no. The house is registered to a business, but I can't find anything about it. I'm guessing it's a shell."

I thought about what Abigail had said about Barry. "I think a dealer owns the house—his name might be Barry. Can you see if you can find anything about somebody named Barry associated with the company?"

"I'll try—"

"And Larissa—"

"They have proof she didn't leave the apartment that morning!" Kim was sounding exasperated.

"I know, I just—" It was difficult to put a hunch into words. "I think Larissa knows Barry. Maybe troll her social media and if you find a Barry, you will have a last name to work with."

"Sure, she couldn't possibly know more than one person named Barry." Kim chuckled. "What are you going to do when I'm out of this cast and not sitting on the computer all day to do your work?"

"I guess I will just have to stop investigating murders."

18

Conscious of the fact that I was about to demand an audience with a drug dealer and potential killer, I sent two quick messages—one to Kim and one to Jake— "Going to Larissa's; call me in an hour if I don't call first."

I pounded on the door.

Larissa opened it with a scowl on her face. "You, again." I pushed myself by her and into the apartment. "You can't—"

"I can." I wasn't about to let her stop me from finding out who ruined my dream. "We need to talk about Barry."

Her eyes widened at the name, and she shut the door. "What about Barry?"

"Let's start with the fact that he's a drug dealer. And that he was fired from the swanky rehab you attended because he was selling to patients." Larissa exhaled and pointed me to a seat in the living room. "Now, those are known facts in the case. The rest... the rest is still coming together, but I think that you are a dealer, too, and that is why Sarah ended up dead."

"No!" For the first time, Larissa showed an emotion that wasn't anger or disdain. "Barry is a Big Man and I sell for him. I'm not gonna lie about it. So what? But he didn't have anything to do with—I didn't have anything to do with—Casey's death." Her breath hitched. "She was my best friend."

I studied Larissa carefully, trying to decide if she was being truthful or trying to scam me. "Who was she hiding from in Austin?"

"It doesn't matter." Larissa refused to meet my gaze. "She couldn't stay inside, and they found her, so we had to move her again."

"Why not just speak to her parents and get it over with? Get a restraining order or something?"

She lifted her face, a smirk in place. "She didn't care about her parents."

"I don't believe you were home when Sarah was killed."

The smirk turned into a smile. "I wasn't."

My heart pounded. "You did kill her!"

"No," a softness once again appeared on her face. "I'd never hurt her. I was making a sale at the gas station at Pecan and Watson."

"Inside?"

"No, outside. Pump 8. I fill up and wash the windows. Buyer pulls up at Pump 7, on the other side of me, and we do the deal right there."

"Then you'll be on security video?"

She leaned back, crossing her long legs in front of her. "I'd suspect so. You can share it with the police, but they won't have enough to go on. I'm not stupid." She glanced around the apartment. "And I have great lawyers."

I stood to exit. "I am sharing this with the police, so you can expect a visit. I am not afraid of you."

Larissa stood and walked to open the door for me. "You don't need to be afraid of me. I have no reason to hurt you. But someone does, and if you keep snooping around about Casey—"

She closed the door, the final words left unsaid.

EVEN THOUGH I was sure Larissa was a terrible person, I was also sure she didn't murder Sarah. Her body language changed whenever she talked about her—Sarah really was her best friend. I decided to swing by my house before going to Andy with the information from my encounter with Larissa. There was no telling how long he'd interrogate me this time, and tomorrow was going to be a long day.

I parked my car at the street and, out of lifelong habit, headed around the house to the back door. My phone pinged as I passed the pecan tree. I scrolled through the message from Jake—"It's been an hour, are you okay?" I thumbed up the message and started tapping out a reply when the phone rang with a call from Kim. I answered as I shifted things in my hands to unlock the door.

I caught a glimpse of movement from the neighbor's cat and—

"IT'S OKAY, Pops, they're on the way." I opened my eyes to see two Aarons hovering above me. I closed my eyes again. "Stay with me…" I tried to mumble a response, only to be shushed by the Aarons. "You don't need to talk, just squeeze my hand and let me know you are here."

I WAS FINALLY able to tell Andy about Larissa when he interviewed me from my hospital bed. After, of course, he bawled me out for doing all the things that got him the information that might lead to a break in the major cases—really the only cases—in Baseless.

The two Aarons? Thank goodness there was only one, the

second the result of the concussion—a gift from the neigh-bor's cat. No, wait, that's not right. It wasn't the neighbor's cat. I saw the neighbor's cat and then something—someone—hit me from the side. They knocked me to the ground, and I smashed my head against one of the terra cotta pots housing my kitchen herb garden. I had just connected with Kim and she heard the commotion, so she yelled for Gabi to call 911. Gabi did, but as any good 14-year-old would do, she was simultaneously using her laptop to share the excitement on social media. And Cam, being a 15-year-old boy with lots of work to do, was sitting in the grass behind the brewery scrolling on his phone when he saw the update. He found Aaron, who then beat the ambulance to my house by three minutes. Not long after the paramedics had whisked me away, Jake went looking for me at the taproom and he got the news. He was the last to arrive but managed to find his way to the emergency room.

And they were all there as I was wheeled out of my room, ready to be sent home.

"I—um—does anyone have my phone?" I was still a little groggy, whether from the terra cotta pot or the pain meds, I wasn't sure.

Andy stepped forward. "The crime lab has it. Whoever attacked you stomped on it a couple of times." He let out a long sigh. "I'm glad it was just the phone."

"Oh, I just… I was gonna call an Uber. I don't remember where I left my car."

Cam snickered and received a harsh look from Aaron and… well, just everyone.

"I'll take you home," Jake offered.

"No!" The assembled crowd spoke over one another as they determined who should drive me where.

I mouthed "thank you" to Jake and motioned for the aide to follow him to the parking lot.

"You really should have someone to help you at home,"

the aide said, "at least for the next 24 hours. You may have some dizziness and altered thinking."

I closed my eyes to get rid of the roller-coaster feeling from the ride across the parking lot. "I'll be fine, thank you." I slid into the passenger side of Jake's car. "Home, please."

My simple ride home became a parade from the hospital to my house. Jake's car led, followed by Aaron and Cam, who were followed by Papi driving Mami, Kim, and the girls, and bringing up the rear was Andy, in his cruiser. I guess I should just be thankful that Andy didn't turn on the lights and siren.

"You know," Jake pondered as he drove slowly through the neighborhood streets. "I want to find out what happened to Sarah, but I'm really worried about you."

"I'm fine, it's just a bump on the head."

"Someone attacked you, Poppy!" His voice had an edge to it. "You need to leave this alone. Forget about Sarah, forget about everything, before you end up just like her."

The slow-moving parade pulled up in front of my house. "I appreciate that you're worried. I just need some sleep and we can talk about this tomorrow."

"Sure, sure," He jumped up and ran around to open the door and help me make my way up to the front door. "Listen, the hospital said you need help. I can sleep on your cou—"

"No." Aaron shook through his keys until he found the emergency key to my house. "I'm staying."

I leaned against the doorjamb for support, my head pounding and stomach roiling. "No, you're not."

Kim stood at the bottom of the steps and called up. "Quit being idiots, I will stay with her!"

Andy yelled back at her, "Who is being an idiot? You can't even get up the steps by yourself, how are you going to help her?"

Another round of arguing ensued.

"Hey!" I yelled, the word echoing in my head. "I just want to go in and get some sleep. I don't need a babysitter. No one is sleeping on my couch. I will be the only person in the house. I love you all, now go away."

"At least let me sweep the house once before you go in." I nodded my assent to Andy and closed my eyes as I listened to the surrounding voices. Cam and Gabi chatted quietly on the sidewalk, while Lexi giggled around them. Jake had moved over to the cars and was conversing with Mami and Papi in smooth Spanish, charming them in the same way he did our customers each morning. Aaron and Kim muttered, both somehow angry that Andy was allowed in the house and they were not.

Andy finally re-emerged from the house and declared it free of boogey-monsters. I didn't even hang around to watch the parade make its final round, I just locked the door behind me and went straight to bed.

19

My body felt like lead. My head was heavy, but I was no longer experiencing shooting pain behind my eyeballs with every step. I drug myself into the shower, then managed to swallow two acetaminophens before making my way to the kitchen. I opened the back door to survey the scene of the crime. It looked like it did when I walked up yesterday afternoon. I could only spot two differences—a smear of blood on a terra cotta pot where I'd gone down, and Aaron curled up in the fetal position, asleep on the wicker loveseat.

I poked at his shoulder. "Do I need to call the police and report a trespasser?"

He stirred, wiping the of drool from the corner of his mouth, then sat up, stretching his long legs from their cramped position. "No, they're already out front."

I left him sitting and marched through the house and out to the front door to the cruiser parked by the sidewalk. I pounded on the window. "I said I didn't want anyone staying here!"

Andy startled awake at the sound and struggled to open the door. He finally pulled himself out of the car and squinted at me through the morning sun. "We stayed outside. Technically, I'm on city property, so you don't have any say. If you want me to call Cleary to come pick up Aaron for trespassing, I'll do that."

"I just need a phone to call for a ride to work."

Aaron came around the corner of the house, very much looking like he'd spent a restless night on a wicker loveseat. "You don't need to go anywhere."

"I know Bluebonnet doesn't officially start until tomorrow, but the crowds are starting. I may not have a food truck, but I've prepped for the crowds. If I'm not serving this weekend, that is money down the drain." A sudden thought hit me. "Why are you here? This is a huge weekend for the taproom! Get out!"

Aaron shook his head. "No. Not until you agree to let someone stay with you."

I changed tactics. "If you give me a ride to the taphouse, you can keep an eye on me all day."

Andy stepped in. "The ER said you need to rest—"

The rest of his words were shut behind the slamming door of my house.

I made a mental note to have a landline installed in the house as I used my laptop to send a message to Jake. "I need a ride to work today. Can you pick me up?"

"Umm, we're working? Pick you up in an hour."

As I suspected, Andy and Aaron were not happy to see Jake pull up. We repeated the small parade from the night before, this time from my house to the crowded parking lot at St. Andrew's Brewery. A few visitors milled about, but most of the crowd consisted of vendors and city workers putting on the final touches for the weekend.

Jake was not nearly as annoying as Andy and Aaron, but

he still couldn't help but to mansplain. "You're in a dangerous situation, Poppy. Getting too close is dangerous—you could have been killed yesterday."

"I know I'm getting close—that's why I can't stop!"

Jake put the car in park and his features went dark as he turned to me. "Stay out of it."

Unsettled by his sudden change in mood, I nodded weakly and made my way to the kitchen. I set about to work, hoping to clear my mind with the mundane tasks before me. I stationed myself working on burger toppings and put Jake on the fry slicer. So many fries. It would have been much easier to buy pre-sliced, frozen potatoes, and most people wouldn't notice (or care)—but I would. Instead, Jake carted 40-pound bags of large potatoes from the outside walk-in to the kitchen where he scrubbed, peeled, and sliced them, dropped into tubs of baking soda water and carted them back to the walk-in. A dance that would be repeated many times over the weekend.

Mid-way through the morning, Deidre came out of the office and handed me a message from Andy. "Video confirms Larissa at gas station. Getting warrant for apartment. Be careful."

I folded the pink note and slipped it into my pocket, Jake watching my every move. "Everything okay?" he asked.

I nodded, unsure if I should share the information about his friend. "They finally have a break."

He stopped his work and gave me a questioning look. "Who has a break?"

"Andy," I searched for the right words, my head still swimming from my close encounter with the terra cotta pot. "I mean, DPS, or whoever. They've got Larissa selling drugs on video—"

"You don't know when to stop, do you?"

This was not how I expected things to go. "Aren't you glad? That's probably the missing piece in solving—"

"What makes you think that? Ris has been selling since she was 14; Casey never touched drugs."

"But—" I stopped; the words gone. Something wasn't right, but I couldn't make the connections.

Jake stepped closer to me and I inched back, feeling a sudden need for space. "I liked you, Poppy, I really did. I tried to warn you—"

"I'm okay, I'm okay!" I continued to creep backward. "You don't understand—Larissa knew that Sarah's parents found her in Austin—"

Jake laughed, and a chill ran across me. "Are you really that stupid? Casey's parents didn't find her—you delivered her to them."

"Why are you calling her Casey?"

"That's her name. She's always been Casey, no matter how many times she tried to hide."

The pieces started to connect. "How did you know where to take me home last night?"

A cold smile creased his face. "I followed that cop."

"No, that's not right. Andy was behind us, behind everyone. You knew where you were going."

He shrugged his shoulders and placed his hands against the wall, caging me in. "You might be smarter than I thought. But still not smart enough to know when to shut up."

"Are you Barry?"

He laughed, and I saw my opportunity to run, but he caught me around my waist and threw me back against the wall. "I told you, I'm done with drugs. Ris can mess with that all she wants, but I'm clean. I got clean for Casey, but then she was going to leave anyway."

"Sarah wasn't going to leave—she was going to work full time for me!"

"Full-time for you means no time for her Chulo, her Papi." He lifted the sleeve to show an elaborate tattoo on his left forearm. A pin-up girl with the words "Papi Chulo" above and "Casey" below.

"You—" he moved his forearm across my throat and leaned into the wall. "You're Pa—" Sparks flew across my darkening eyes as I tried to get the words out.

My breath returned in a gasp and I heard a familiar voice yelling, "Run, run!"

So, I did.

A forty-pound sack of potatoes across the back will put a person down for a while, but not long. I ran out the back door of the kitchen and snaked through the vendors setting up. I had no idea where I was or where I was going, and I hoped Jake didn't either. On my last turn, I ran into an immovable object. Fortunately, it was in the form of Mr. Martin.

"Poppy, what in the world are you doing?"

I gasped for breath, still looking behind my shoulder. "It's Jake. He's Papi. He did it."

Mr. Martin led me into a nearby vendor booth and sat me down while he had 911 on the line. "That kid Jake that works in the food truck. I don't know what Poppy's going on about, but you need to find him, and now."

20

It didn't take long for them to find Jake—Andy was already on the way to the taphouse before the call was made. While viewing the tape of Larissa at the gas station he noticed something else—Jake driving by. But they already had video of Jake driving by the gas station as he circled back to take Sarah her phone. They discovered he made the loop twice—just long enough for him to leave the scene and return after Sarah had already bled out. They had some questions for him.

Mr. Martin agreed to let me serve out of the taphouse during Bluebonnet Trails if I would serve as kitchen director and let his crew do the behind-the-scenes work. I happily complied.

Will Wrigley sat at the bar, Lone Star Burger in front of him. "I'm so sorry I wasn't there earlier."

"Please, Will, don't apologize for saving my life!" I looked at the small man, still flabbergasted that he had hoisted a forty-pound bag of potatoes above his head and launched it at Jake's back. "You are my hero." Aaron cleared the classes next to Will and snorted. I rolled my eyes and spoke to Will. "Ignore him. He's just upset that he didn't figure it out."

"I do wish," Will swallowed a large bite of burger. "That I'd put the pieces together sooner. I was sure the girl was involved in drugs, but I didn't see how sweet Sarah could have been party to that."

"Well," I nibbled on a fry from his plate. "She wasn't. She knew Larissa was dealing, but as long as she wasn't using, she didn't care. It's funny, the exceptions people will make for friends."

"Indeed." Will glanced toward Aaron. "What have we learned about the young man who tried to choke the life out of you?"

I shuddered, remembering how close I'd come to being another one of Jake's victims. "He was being truthful about being clean. Unfortunately, he couldn't let go of Sarah—that's why she'd changed her name twice, she was hiding from him, not her parents. He was obsessed."

"And that obsession cost the dear child her life."

I nodded. "She had taken him back after he got out of rehab. She thought he'd be different. Maybe he thought he could be different, too. He wanted her to be with him, with no friends or passions of her own. In his twisted mind he decided he was better off without her than sharing her with the world."

William took a long drink. "Now I understand why he was so insistent that I was stalking her."

"The whole sad story is coming together, but I there is one thing I still don't know—"

"I sent it." Will dropped his eyes to his plate. "The benefit of being an invisible man is that you get lots of information just by standing around. Unfortunately, it's not always the right pieces. I thought Larissa might be a danger to you."

"Why didn't you just tell me?"

"It's awfully rude just to accuse someone with nothing to back it up."

Aaron snorted again, but I continued to ignore him. "In

the future, know that you can just talk to me—you don't have to send an anonymous note."

Andy entered the taproom and Aaron shouted across to him. "Hey, Trooper Gomez, what can I get you today? A go-cup of our finest IPA?"

"Hilarious, Aaron," he removed his Stetson and stepped up to the bar. "That's a great way to get me suspended while they investigate me for drinking on the job." He sat next to Will and sipped from the iced tea I placed in front of him. "I thought you'd like to know that Larissa has been denied bail."

Aaron, Will, and I all stopped what we were doing and turned our attention to Andy. "Really?"

"Yep, the state lab is running some tests right now, but there's a good chance she supplied the drugs that killed Rhys Gilley. She was selling to some other kids at the high school and once word got out that she'd been arrested, they suddenly decided confession was good for the soul."

"Is that really enough to be denied bail?"

"That and she has the means to take off somewhere without extradition." Andy tapped his fingers on the bar. "She might help her case if she gives up her supplier, and if she testifies against Jake."

I drew in a quick breath. "Did she know Jake was the one who killed Sarah?!"

"No," Andy responded. "She didn't know, but she suspected. He'd met Sarah—Casey then—when they were teens in Lubbock. He'd been obsessed with her ever since. Larissa was afraid of what he might do to her she talked." He sighed and stood up from the bar. "The important thing is that you are safe."

I smiled at him, my mood lightening for the first time in a month. "And I have learned my lesson—I'll keep cooking and leave the investigating to the professionals!"

I heard his voice coming from the other end of the bar. "Excuse me, I'm looking for Poppy Price—"

Aaron's reply was terse. "You can leave a message with me—"

I strained to see who he was talking to, then ran around the bar to my target. "Roger!"

He lifted me off the floor in a bear hug, then placed me back on my feet, examining the marks on my head and neck. "I got worried when you stopped responding to my messages, so I came down on check on you."

"Oh, my phone!" I reached for in my back pocket, where it usually rested. "It's, umm, well... I need a new one. There was an accident."

"But you," he pushed my hair away to better see my bruise. "You're okay?"

I took his hand and smiled. "Now I am."

Lone Star Burgers with Cilantro Pecan Pesto and Crunchy Southwestern Relish

Cilantro Pecan Pesto
    1 bunch cilantro
    2 cloves garlic
    3-4 tablespoons olive oil
    1/2 cup toasted pecans
    1 tablespoon fresh lime juice
    1/8 teaspoon ground black pepper
    1/4 teaspoon salt

Olive oil for brushing on grill

Patties
    2 large poblano peppers, roasted, peeled, seeded and finely chopped
    2 tablespoons butter
    1/2 cup pecans, minced
    2 teaspoons salt
    2 pounds ground chuck
    1/4 cup Belgian-style blonde ale

6 slices Pepper Jack Cheese

Cilantro Pecan Pesto Spread
    6 tablespoons mayonnaise
    3 tablespoons cilantro pecan pesto

Crunchy Southwestern Relish

1/3 cup finely chopped red onion

1 medium jicama, peeled and julienned (about 1-1/2 cup strips)

1 medium ripe tomato, seeds and pulp removed, chopped (about 1/2 cup chopped)

1 tablespoon freshly squeezed lime juice

1 large avocado, peeled, pitted and chopped

1/2 teaspoon salt

6 seeded hamburger buns, split

Put cilantro, garlic, olive oil, pecans, lime juice, black pepper, and salt into a blender or food processor. Process on high until paste is formed. Cover and set aside.

Preheat grill to medium-high.

When grill is ready, brush the grill rack with olive oil. Place the poblano peppers directly onto the hottest part of the grill rack. Turn as needed to char all sides of the peppers. When sides are charred, remove from grill and place in a sealable, food safe plastic bag. Close bag and allow peppers to steam for about 10 to 15 minutes. When pepper has steamed, remove from bag and pull charred skin off pepper. Carefully remove stem and seeds. Chop pepper and place into a large bowl.

While pepper is charring, place butter and pecans into a small grill safe skillet over medium heat area and stir occasionally until pecans are toasted. Set aside to cool.

To make patties, add salt, beef, ale, and toasted pecans to bowl containing poblano peppers. Handling the meat as little as possible to avoid compacting it, mix well. Divide the mixture into 6 equal portions and form the portions into patties slightly larger than the rolls. Do not press the patties tightly together. Cover patties and refrigerate for about 15 minutes.

To make spread, mix mayonnaise and 3 tablespoons pesto together in a small bowl. Cover and refrigerate until ready to assemble burgers. Cover remaining pesto and refrigerate for future use.

To make relish while patties chill, in a medium bowl mix together red onion, jicama, tomato, lime juice, avocado, and salt. Cover and set aside.

Brush additional olive oil on grill. Place the patties on the rack, cover, and cook, turning once, until done to preference, about 5 to 7 minutes on each side for medium. Add cheese slices to patty tops for melting a couple of minutes before cooking time is finished. During the last few minutes of cooking, place the rolls, cut side down, on the sides of the grill rack to lightly toast.

To assemble burgers, spread roll bottoms with equal portions of cilantro spread and add a cheese topped patty to each. With a slotted spoon, place equal portions of the relish on top of each patty. Add the roll tops and serve. Makes 6 burgers.

We hope you've enjoyed your time in Baseless—Deep in the heart of Texas, where mayhem and mysteries roam. To keep the stories coming, please consider the following:

- Leave a review on your favorite book site
- Tell a friend about Poppy's adventures and author Moira Bates
- Ask your local library to put Moira's work on the shelf
- Recommend Fawkes Press books to your local bookstore

Thanks for making great books possible!

WWW.MOIRABATESMYSTERIES.COM
WWW.FAWKESPRESS.COM / NEWSLETTER

FAWKES PRESS

Made-up for Murder: Mid-Life Mysteries #1

"You do the crime; you do the time."

Julia Melvin had repeated those words countless times as she raised her children, proud to be teaching them personal responsibility. She did not expect to hear them parroted back from her young adult son on her *one* phone call from the county jail following a small skirmish at a protest against animal testing at a local cosmetics company.

Upon her release she vowed to change her criminal ways and stay far away from the protest site. And she did. Kind of. Mostly. She just wanted to help the animals. How was she supposed to know she'd stumble over the dead body of the company owner? Now she's got two criminal cases pending and is doing all she can to avoid having murder added to her ever-growing rap sheet.

Fans of Agatha Raisin will love forty-something and fierce Julia Jane Melvin. Mid-Life Mysteries do not contain graphic violence, gore, strong language, or cliffhangers.

AVAILABLE EVERYWHERE MAY 31, 2021

CPSIA information can be obtained
at www.ICGtesting.com
Printed in the USA
LVHW091204060521
686680LV00010B/713